HANNIE RAYSON is a graduate of the University of Melbourne and the Victorian College of the Arts (VCA). She holds an Honorary Doctorate of Letters from La Trobe University, and is a Fellow of the Australian Centre, University of Melbourne. Rayson was a cofounder of Theatreworks, and has served as writer-in-residence at the Mill Theatre, Playbox Theatre, La Trobe University, Monash University, VCA and New Writing North (Newcastle-upon-Tyne, UK).

Her plays have been performed extensively around Australia and several have been produced overseas. For Theatreworks she wrote *Please Return to Sender* (1980) and *Mary* (1981). *Leave It Till Monday* (1984) was first produced by the Mill Theatre. *Room to Move* (1985) won the Australian Writers' Guild AWGIE Award for Best Original Stage Play. *Hotel Sorrento* (Playbox / Theatreworks 1990) also won an AWGIE, a NSW Premier's Literary Award and the Green Room Award for Best Play. A feature film of *Hotel Sorrento* (1995) won two Australian Film Institute Awards, including Best Screenplay. *Falling from Grace* (Playbox, 1994) won a NSW Premier's Literary Award and the *Age* Performing Arts Award. *Scenes From A Separation,* co-written with Andrew Bovell, was produced by the Melbourne Theatre Company in 1985, the Sydney Theatre Company in 2004 and The Orange Tree Theatre UK in 2005. Her satire on the deregulation in local government, *Competitive Tenderness*, premiered at Playbox in 1996. Her examination of the corporatisation of universities, *Life After George* (2000) enjoyed separate productions by the Melbourne Theatre Company and the Sydney Theatre Company. It was nominated for the NSW and Queensland Premier's Literary Awards, and won a Victorian Premier's Literary Award, the Green Room Award for Best New Australian Play, and two Helpmann Awards for the Best New Australian Work and for Best Play. It was also the first play ever to be nominated for the prestigious Miles Franklin Award. *Life After George* has also had major productions on the West End (2002), in Montreal (2003), Vienna and Frankfurt (2004) and The National Theatre of Slovenia (2004). Her rural saga *Inheritance* (MTC 2003) played in Melbourne and Sydney, winning the Helpmann Awards for Best Play and Best New Australian Work. *Two Brothers* (MTC/STC 2005) played to capacity houses at the Melbourne Arts Centre and the Sydney Opera House and then toured in NSW.

Rayson has also written for newspapers and magazines and in 1999 she won the Magazine Publishers' Society of Australia Columnist of the Year Award for her column in *HQ Magazine*. Her television scripts include *Sloth* (ABC, *Seven Deadly Sins*) and she co-wrote two episodes of the award-winning series *SeaChange* (ABC/Artists Services).

Diane Craig as Fiona and Garry McDonald as Eggs
in the 2005 STC / MTC production. (Photo: Jeff Busby)

Two Brothers

HANNIE RAYSON

CURRENCY PRESS

CURRENCY PLAYS

First published in 2005
by Currency Press Pty Ltd,
PO Box 2287, Strawberry Hills, NSW, 2012, Australia
enquiries@currency.com.au
www.currency.com.au

Reprinted 2011, 2012, 2013, 2015, 2020

NATIONAL LIBRARY OF AUSTRALIA CIP DATA
Rayson, Hannie, 1957–.
Two brothers.
ISBN 9780868197814.
I. Title. (Series: Currency plays).
A822.3

Set by Dean Nottle
Cover design by Kate Florance for Currency Press
Front cover shows Garry McDonald as Eggs and Nicholas Eadie as Tom in the 2005 STC / MTC production of *Two Brothers*. Photo: Jeff Busby

Currency Press acknowledges the Traditional Owners of the Country on which we live and work. We pay our respects to all Aboriginal and Torres Strait Islander Elders, past and present.

Contents

Political Fictions

Katharine Brisbane

Whichever way you look at it *Two Brothers* is a problem play. In writing it Hannie Rayson sought to investigate a perceived problem. In the process this created reverberations for the theatres that commissioned it; for the actors that performed it; for the University of Melbourne that supported it; the Australia Council which, as the Federal Government's arts funding body, was responsible for it; and finally for the Coalition Cabinet that was hurt by it. Or so the story goes.

Two Brothers is a thriller which, within the parameters of dramatic entertainment, poses some moral questions: when power is in your hands, how far will ideology and personal ambition drive you? Does the end ever justify the means? In order to argue this the author creates two brothers, opposite in temperament and outlook but linked by strong family ties. One is a prime minister-in-waiting who believes any means are justifiable if your aim is the common good; and the other the head of a charitable foundation who believes that good can only be achieved by acting with a clear conscience. In the writing, says the author, she drew on her relationship with her brother, whose political views differ markedly from her own, even though they shared the same upbringing. She has also admitted that the plot was inspired by the Costello brothers, Peter, Federal Treasurer and prime minister-in-waiting; and the Rev. Tim, CEO of World Vision.

And there's the rub. The debut production made of the play a triumph and tragedy of marketing. The thought of a major political figure being portrayed on stage as ruthlessly ambitious, adulterous, a neglectful father and husband, responsible for mass and individual killings, was too good to resist. The press—the news desks and columnists, that is— had a field day. The reviewers confined themselves to the performance. Next time perhaps the theatres will not be so meticulous in providing their audiences with historical background in their programs.

I have not seen the play in performance, but I read it when the scandal broke. And saw in the manuscript little that could relate to the barrage of personal abuse to which performance exposed it. Let me say at once that on the page 'Eggs' and Tom Benedict in no way resemble the Costello brothers. Nor would anyone, even those who know them only by reputation, as I do, find anything in common between the real and the fictional except their positions in life. Eggs is the classic hero-villain who brings about his own downfall: a hard-bitten pragmatist whose determination to keep control of a spiralling disaster is bound to lead to family break-up and violence. Tom is an open-hearted family man, rich in both sensuality and altruism. These are the driving dramatic forces behind the play. They have nothing to do with the personal history of a living family.

But they have been taken personally. As the journalist David Marr said in his Philip Parsons Memorial Lecture in Sydney on 9 October 2005:

So stung was the Government by *Two Brothers*, that a debate began among senior ministers about abolishing the Australia Council. The military was particularly enraged. As it happens, a number of arts budget proposals were sitting on Peter Costello's desk when all this blew up. But John Howard calmed this behind-the-scenes debate down. The proposals went through. But [Assistant Treasurer Rod] Kemp made the displeasure of the Government known to the general managers of the Melbourne Theatre Company and the Sydney Theatre Company. He also spoke to the chair of the MTC—and now Chancellor of Melbourne University—Ian Reynard. According to reports, the Minister said to Reynard: 'Why do you persist in biting the hand that feeds?'

Kemp does not deny making his feelings known at the time. He told me: 'The generally poor reviews by critics across the political spectrum suggest that *Two Brothers* was more of a political rant than a significant contribution to Australian theatre and political commentary. Equally, comments by those closely associated with the play that it wasn't aimed at particular individuals were entirely unconvincing.'

On ABC-TV's *Insiders*, Barrie Cassidy asked the Treasurer if he were annoyed by the thinly disguised portrait of him in the play. He was. 'What else can they say about you: mass killer, serial adulterer? You know, in some sections of the theatre anyone who votes Liberal is just considered fair game.' So what could the arts industry look forward to while he was treasurer or prime minister, Cassidy asked. The contender replied: 'I will always make a good subject for their plays, Barry. I would only ask they be a little more accurate in the future.'

'Theatre under Howard',
available on www.currencyhouse.org.au

What this shows is a profound misunderstanding of the traditional role of the theatre. Such a literal reading has understandably produced responses of literal, personal hurt. News desk responses were equally literal and personal, assuming malice aforethought and political bias on the part of the author. Such responses to minority and unpopular opinion have increased as the decade has become more and more empirical, discarding thoughtful argument in favour of pragmatic decisions based on immediate need and political expediency, without reference to future consequence or historical evidence. The public service, the military, the Federal Police, have each in turn been observed to act with such expediency. Charities have been put on notice; the arm's length principle of the Australia Council has been challenged. Why should art and literature be immune from the fear of retaliation for giving offence?

Parliamentarians do not, on the whole, read fiction, according to the summer reading lists, though thrillers are a popular airport pastime. And we are talking about a thriller here. The trouble is that Rayson has chosen to invade the empiricists' territory, to relate her fiction to recent events of which we still have emotional memory; and there are grounds for criticism in its accusation that the Royal Australian Navy broke the law of the sea by deserting drowning people on the order of a minister of state. Tony Kevin in his introduction has written about that evidence and the probability of the play's story being true to life. As he demonstrates, enough grey area still remains in the SIEV X affair on which to build a fiction. History will judge whether the story has the ring of moral truth, whether the characters are believable, whether the outcome is inevitable, long after the details of the SIEV X tragedy have faded. What will remain of the historical events themselves is a corporate memory of something shameful that occurred, something that we did not understand but which damaged our view of ourselves as an honourable nation. That is much more important in the long run than personal hurt about personal matters. Our country's leaders must be big enough to recognise that. That is why we elected them to lead us.

The British, on which we have modelled both our government and our drama, would have had no problem with this. From Shakespeare's time their writers ran a fine line between libel and allegory as regimes changed. Censorship arrived with constitutional government and was as quickly traduced. And in more recent times their governments have cohabited mildly, if not happily, with TV shows like *Yes, Minister*, *House of Cards* and more recently the no-holds-barred *Spooks*, which accuses the British Government of criminal behaviour the like of which Eggs Benedict could never have imagined.

What Hannie Rayson has done is give us fair warning. The play is set in the future so we have time to stay the course. If we allow ourselves to make political expediency the grounds for today's decisions, without proper consideration of tomorrow, then we well might find ourselves, as Eggs does, betraying family, beliefs and country. And if Tom allows family feeling and goodwill to blind him to the vulnerable position in which he has placed his asylum-seeker clients and his foundation, then he too is in the way of facing a massive compromise.

The Iago of the play is, in fact, not Eggs but Jamie Savage, the Minister's personal assistant. And the Desdemona is his son Lachlan, the innocent young naval officer who adores the Navy's noble history but is disillusioned and sacrificed. Othello, in this saga, is both Eggs and Tom, two sides of a man betrayed by his own weakness. For it is Jamie, the stop-at-nothing manipulator, who achieves her end, while for her victims everything that matters is lost. Jamie is the sinister side of Sir Humphrey Appleby and she leaves Eggs without a will of his own. Will she remain as head of her Prime Minister's Department I wonder? Perhaps, like Humphrey, she will outstay him.

Two Brothers has brought to a head a rising awareness of bureaucratic- and self- censorship in the arts about which hitherto there has been silence. The Australia Council is caught in this net as a responsible patron and lobbyist for recipients perceived by its sponsors as recalcitrant. A healthy society needs the healthy exchange of ideas, robust challenges, as well as vested interests and political will and we look to the humanities to supply this. My lasting impression of *Two Brothers* is its realisation of an existential time, a time of division, fear and moral bankruptcy in which two families attempt feebly to hold together without social or spiritual support. This is Australia, the play is saying. Be warned. There are those who would call Hannie Rayson 'courageous' in making this challenge—which in Sir Humphrey's world means foolhardy. I would prefer to believe that as a craftswoman and a fine intellect, she has just been doing her job.

KATHARINE BRISBANE, AM, *was a theatre journalist for 21 years, was publisher of Currency Press until her retirement in 2001, and is author of* Not Wrong Just Different—Observations on the Rise of the Contemporary Australian Theatre *(2005).*

Political Facts

Tony Kevin

The sinking of the SIEV X and the policy of mandatory detention are central to Hannie Rayson's *Two Brothers*. Rayson herself wrote in the play's program:

> On 19 October 2001 a refugee boat sank on its way to Australia— the SIEV X. I began work on this play intending to base the narrative on a true account of the SIEV X but abandoned it because the inconsistencies and obfuscations on the public record make it impossible to know what really happened. Why 353 people drowned when the boat went down in a heavily watched area of ocean is not at all transparent. The dimensions of this tragedy—and the unnerving sense that we are not being told the whole truth—are compounded by our cruel treatment of asylum seekers, by the inhumanity of the 'Pacific Solution' and by mandatory detention.

The play cleverly links the two issues through the character of Hazem who survived the sinking of Rayson's fictional boat, the *Kelepasan*. He had previously gone through the detention centre processing in Australia to be granted a Temporary Protection Visa, the conditions of which he violated in order to fly back to Indonesia to accompany his family on the boat. It is a hauntingly powerful idea.

It is based on fact. At least one man, Zainalabaden Aluomer, who was in Australia on a Temporary Protection Visa, flew back to Indonesia voluntarily in order to accompany his wife and children here. He died with them on SIEV X. Perhaps there were others, too. And perhaps there are bereaved men in Australia who reproach themselves still for not going.

Although it is a fictional work, in its political context, Rayson's play is right on the money. Indeed, as I watched the play, I had an unnerving sense of my personal SIEV X experience being rolled out before me. Words I had recorded, statements of fact I had heard or read in the Senate Certain Maritime Incident (CMI) Committee Hansard were echoed in Rayson's crisp dialogue. For example, the fictional survivor Hazem Al Ayad's harrowing account of the fictional boat sinking draws heavily on the recorded statements of survivors in Bogor after the SIEV X disaster. Eggs Benedict's son, naval officer Lachlan Benedict, expresses his conflict between duty and conscience in words that reflect the experiences of real people who, like Lachlan, were under orders from Canberra. These include Commander Norman Banks of HMAS Adelaide in the SIEV 4 interception, the crew of HMAS Tobruk and Dr Duncan Wallace, RAN Naval Reserve psychologist serving on HMAS Arunta, the closest ship to SIEV X when it sank, according to Australian Defence Force evidence at the Senate CMI enquiry.

All this gives the play enormous authenticity and credibility, and it leads me to wonder why so many critics were determined to deny Rayson this authenticity. Like my book on SIEV X, *Two Brothers* was targeted from the beginning by efforts to discredit it. The whole unpleasant experience must have given Rayson and the Melbourne Theatre Company some anxious moments. A lot had been invested in this play and its success in the marketplace. The warning sent to Rayson and to others who might be tempted to heed her play's message was, I believe, unambiguous: go down this road and we will try to destroy you. The critical reception tells us much about the current intimidated climate of intellectual and moral debate in Australia.

The play opened on 13 April 2005. On that same day Andrew Bolt wrote the first of two violent diatribes against the play and against Rayson personally, 'Shameful Saga of Hate' in Melbourne's *Herald-Sun*. For example:

> If you still need proof of how far up its own fundament our artists have crawled, go to tonight's premiere of Hannie Rayson's play, 'Two Brothers'… this vomit of smug hate… see how cruelly and hysterically she [Rayson] smears our defence personnel, and anyone who even votes Liberal.

He followed up this remarkable (even by his own standards) piece two days later, again in the *Herald-Sun*, with 'Hannie's evil brew', which included an unsubtle warning that most of Rayson's artistic work had been financed by national arts subsidies and implying that all this could now be at risk:

> So how has she been able to keep distant all these fellow Australians, all those potential theatregoers, without at least going broke from lack of ticket sales? And why does she so hate or fear these non-Leftists?
>
> I suspect it's that flood of government gold that allows Rayson to drink and drink, without having to ask nicely for water from the passing crowd instead. That great gush of public money that makes our guzzling artists praise the Lord for big government of the Left and fear the Liberal demons who might turn off that tap, and point them to their public.
>
> See for yourself how government cash has trained, paid, feted, nursed and staged Rayson or her works, making the public's verdict indecisive, if not irrelevant...

This is savage stuff—the sort of smear that the play's character Jamie Savage might have placed with supportive media people to protect her employer's interests. And Bolt's words bring to mind a key moment in the play when Jamie warns Tom Benedict that the funding of his social welfare organisation will be at risk if he continues to stir up trouble for the government on refugee issues.

Other critics argued that Rayson, a playwright of acknowledged and deserved high repute, had failed in her attempt to tackle perhaps the biggest moral issue in Australia today—the cruel treatment of boat people and people in detention centres. (Many of these reviews can be read on Marg Hutton's website www.sievx.com) Various reasons were advanced for why she had failed. Tom Hyland in the *Age*, for example, attacked the play's many departures from factual reality, concluding: 'It's a pity Rayson has ignored another political truism: truth is the best propaganda'.

In response, Rayson stressed that her play is a work of fiction:

> Writing a play is different from writing a piece of investigative journalism. In Tom Hyland's attack on my play (Opinion, 15/4), he writes that *Two Brothers* is 'a compelling, provocative and entertaining dramatic thriller'. But apparently, that is not enough. According to Hyland, I've written a terrific play—but it fails

because it is not a factual account of what happened to the SIEV X, the refugee boat that sank on its way to Australia on October 19, 2001.

Some critics argued that the play's central character Eggs Benedict lacked the complexity to make him an interesting villain, ignoring the dramatic tension played out in the responses of his horrified family members to his manipulative strategies. Yet we see Eggs' contradictions in the early hours of the morning, when he cannot sleep. He is tormented by thoughts of what he has done. This places him squarely in Richard III villain territory. But in waking hours, he is no tortured Macbeth (although his coldly ruthless adviser and lover, Jamie Savage, comes closer to Lady Macbeth). Rather Eggs plays a seemingly weak hand with great coolness, and in the end wins.

Had any member of his family called his bluff, Eggs would not become Prime Minister. But none do so. His wife Fiona reverts to long-practised submission, after a brief flirtation with revolt. His idealistic brother Tom and wife Ange cave in at the prospect of a fifteen-year jail sentence for their son Harry on drug charges engineered by Eggs and Jamie. Eggs' own son Lachlan submits, too, recognising that his sense of filial loyalty matters more to him than his public ethics. They succumb one by one to his blackmail and bribes. As Helen Thomson, drama critic for the Melbourne *Age*, observed in her laudatory review, the play 'skilfully condensed and dramatised a national narrative into a family drama, making the political intensely personal'.

This is a bleak vision of how evil triumphs when good people for whatever reason do nothing, or not enough to make the difference. Rather than being a one-sided account, the play symbolises the complex reality of life. Hundreds of people with some real knowledge of what happened to the SIEV X must have faced similar dilemmas of conscience and career to those portrayed in the play. In four years, they have said nothing. Is this, as in the play, the result of a potent combination of service loyalties and fears of punishment? Lachlan, the young naval officer, is one of the most interesting characters in this respect, entirely believable as he swings from blind loyalty to outraged denunciation and finally to acquiescence.

The hinge on which the plot turns—that a RAN vessel witnessed the sinking of a boat but on direct orders from an Australian government minister took no action to rescue survivors in the water—drew fire from many critics as offensive and unbelievable. In relation to SIEV X, one can have the view, as I do, that it is most unlikely that a whole RAN frigate crew would maintain silence for four years about such a grossly unethical and criminal action. Yet the present state of public knowledge does not allow one to definitely rule this out. That is why we need a full judicial inquiry.

More pertinently, this is fiction. It is inevitable for the complexities of real life to be simplified to fit a 90-minute play, and to create plot, action and resolution. The reality, I suspect, is that no single person will ever be found to have ordered, 'Let SIEV X sink—and take no action to save the people'. Instead, it will turn out—like the wrongful apprehension of Cornelia Rau and Vivian Alvarez Solon and other cruel border security-related cases—to have been a complex failure of bureaucratic processes. It is most probably a series of incremental bad or callous information mishandlings and misjudgements in the chain of command, with responsibility diffused among so many people and agencies that in the end no one individual will be really to blame. The truth—the banality of bureaucratic evil—does not make good theatre and *Two Brothers* is gripping theatre.

Yet even if the facts are not as clear-cut as in Rayson's fictional scenario, the play raises possibilities worth airing. This helps explain its success in the theatre where it packed houses, despite the attacks. Some rose to Rayson's defence in print. The *Age* published supportive letters in response to Hyland's article, including letters from Hilary McPhee and myself. I warmly applaud Rayson's courage in writing this fine drama and hope that it will enter into the canon of significant Australian plays. It deserves to be read, studied and performed in years to come.

TONY KEVIN retired from the Department of Foreign Affairs and Trade in 1998 after a 30-year public service career. He is the author of A Certain Maritime Incident: The Sinking of SIEV X.

Two Brothers was first produced by Sydney Theatre Company and Melbourne Theatre Company at the Playhouse, Melbourne, on 13 April 2005 with the following cast:

HAZEM AL AYAD	Rodney Afif
JAMIE SAVAGE	Caroline Brazier
FIONA BENEDICT	Diane Craig
TOM BENEDICT	Nicholas Eadie
ANGELA SIDOROPOULOUS	Laura Lattuada
LACHLAN BENEDICT	Ben Lawson
JAMES 'EGGS' BENEDICT	Garry McDonald
HARRY BENEDICT	Hamish Michael

Director, Simon Phillips
Set Design, Stephen Curtis
Costume Design, Edie Kurzer
Lighting Design, Nick Schlieper
Sound / Composer, Ian McDonald

CHARACTERS

JAMES 'EGGS' BENEDICT, 53, Minister for Home Security

FI BENEDICT, 50, Eggs' wife

LACHLAN BENEDICT, 25, their son, officer in the Navy

TOM BENEDICT, 51, Eggs' brother, Director of the charitable Lawson Foundation

ANGLEA SIDOROPOULOS, 47, Tom's wife, teacher at a western suburbs high school

HARRY BENEDICT, 24, their son, architect

HAZEM AL AYAD, 35, asylum seeker from Iraq

JAMIE SAVAGE, 43, Eggs' senior advisor

ERIC, 40, Eggs' staffer

REPORTERS

THERAPIST

A NOTE ON THE TEXT

Whenever the / symbol appears within the dialogues, it is to indicate that the remainder of the speech is spoken simultaneously with the speech following.

ACT ONE

PROLOGUE

Friday night 8.30 pm. The remote seaside weekender of the Benedict family. The cliff-top house is in darkness. A savage wind is blowing off the sea.

HAZEM *is asleep on the couch.*

Tyres on gravel. A sweep of headlights casts shadows. Footsteps on the gravel. The external light switches on automatically, casting an eerie light in the room. There is the sound of the key in the door. It opens.

As EGGS *reaches for the light switch,* HAZEM *leaps up.* EGGS *shouts out in terror and strikes out at* HAZEM. *The men tumble and flail. Their bodies smash against furniture. A vase smashes to the ground.* EGGS *overpowers him.* EGGS *punches him over and over with a hellish fury; blows to the face and gut.* HAZEM *collapses.*

EGGS *seizes a fishing-knife. He is winded and bleeding.* HAZEM *stirs.* EGGS *lunges at him pointing the knife.*

HAZEM: You!
EGGS: Christ!
HAZEM: You kill my family. Finish the job.

> HAZEM *struggles and is overpowered again.*

EGGS: How the hell did you get in?
HAZEM: You murdered my wife. My children.

> *There is another struggle.*

EGGS: Jesus!
HAZEM: Murderer!

> EGGS *menaces him with the knife at his throat.*

I want the people to know.
EGGS: And how will the people know, my friend? Nobody's watching.

HAZEM *lunges.* EGGS *drives the knife into* HAZEM*'s belly. He folds over and falls to the floor.*

EGGS *stares at the body in horror. He paces around and around the body. He holds his hand out to it, in case it jumps up. As though he is trying to make a point but can't think what it is.*

He begins to hit himself with odd repetitive gestures and mounting aggression.

Get up! Get up! Get up! Get up!

He screams and kicks him.

Do you hear me?! Get up!

He is kicking him repeatedly.

What are you doing here? This is my house. This is your fault. You come here and you try and kill people. [*Pause.*] Whoa. Bleeding. So much bleeding. Hang on. Hang on. Hang on. Hang on. Here. Here. Here. Here.

He runs off and returns with a tea-towel which he scrunches into a ball and pushes tentatively into the wound. Then he springs back and starts to clap his hands together in big spastic claps.

Nope, nope, nope.

He begins to retch and then vomits over the back of the couch. Eventually spent, he reaches for his mobile phone and his composure.

[*Into the mobile*] Jamie? What time is it? Eight-thirty. Okay. Look I'm at the beach house now. How far away are you? No listen, we have a situation.

Outside, it is dark and raining.

◆ ◆ ◆ ◆ ◆

SCENE ONE

Three months earlier.

The rain transforms into applause. The elegant and urbane EGGS BENEDICT *addresses The Melbourne Club. He is fifty-three, bow-tied and nursing a fine glass of red.*

EGGS: Thank you. I have three abiding memories of that night—almost ten years ago now—when you first welcomed me to The Club, as a new member. The first is the splendid curried sausages. Which I've been enjoying ever since.

Laughter. Applause.

The second is the '93 Barkers Hill Cab Sav—which we've laid on again tonight. [*He takes a drink.*] Magnificent.

Gentle laughter. 'Hear, hear.' Applause.

TOM *enters, carrying red wine in a very ordinary wine glass.*

TOM: Thank you, comrades. Last time I addressed the Coburg Branch of the ALP we met in the Edinburgh Arms. I could hardly hear myself speak over the bloody pokies. But this is a very classy act. Good tucker. And Barkers Hill Cab Sav. [*He takes a drink, with the same appreciation displayed by* EGGS.] Lovely.

EGGS: And my third memory is that reprobate Welsford, over there. After pudding, I watched him simultaneously smoke a cigarette, two pipes and an enormous cigar. Dismayed to see you're still with us, Welly.

Laughter. Applause.

TOM: Well, comrades. The conservative jackals are tearing apart every great social reform of the past hundred years. And you know why they're being so ruthless? It's revenge—for the crap time they had at uni in the seventies. They know that we had the best parties and got the best girls.

Laughter. Applause.

EGGS: My friends, thank you for joining me for this little soiree tonight— to celebrate my fifth anniversary as Minister for Home Security.

Applause.

The elegant MRS FI BENEDICT *rises to the applause. It is Speech Night at an exclusive Melbourne girls' school.*

FI: Thank you, Headmistress. Many of you girls will know me through my husband—the Minister for Home Security. But I want you to think of me as part of the Merton Hall family.

EGGS: In a way, the members of a chap's club are like his second family— which, looking at you lot, is a pretty sorry state of affairs.

Laughter.

FI: People sometimes ask—

TOM: People are always asking—

EGGS: People ask me, 'Why do you do it? What's in it for you?'

FI: —'What's it like being a politician's wife?'

TOM: —'How can you possibly speak out so candidly when your brother is the Minister for Home Security?' And the truth is—

EGGS: The truth is—

FI: The truth is, politics is a harsh and unforgiving business.

TOM: —we are both driven to engage with the most divisive struggle facing this country today—

TOM & EGGS: [*together*] The struggle for a fair go.

Applause. Whistles.

ANGELA *enters.*

ANGELA: All right, settle down please, Year Ten. Farouk. We've just got the results from this year's state maths competition. And congratulations go to Fatima Abdulla, Troy Lim and Suzie Lee, who all won Honourable Mentions!

EGGS: A fair go for people with energy and vision.

TOM: For people who are born in some dead-end street—in Melbourne, or Sydney or Afghanistan

EGGS: And the proper role for those of us in government is to get out of the way.

TOM: And we look to government to step in and take responsibility—

EGGS: To make space for those men who have the passion to shape the future.

FI: You girls are the future. You are the adventurers, the dreamers and tomorrow's leaders who we will look to—to run things.

TOM: Now, more than ever, there is a powerful and contemptuous class of men running this country. Running the planet!

EGGS: In a way, running things is small beer, but sharing a sublime moment with a fellow who we know to be clubbable—that is the finest wine of all.

ANGELA: And congratulations to every single one of you who entered: Jim Pappachristos, Franco Priolo, Steve Koutafides, Mohammed Buzek...

EGGS: Each of you has made a remarkable success of his life. Together, you are a bloody inspiration—

ANGELA: … Diem Quoc, Thuy Quoc, Slobodan Jevic…

EGGS: Because today, all energy and vigour is coming from our side of politics.

TOM: They're not interested in democracy.

EGGS: This government has, I believe, acted with extraordinary courage—

TOM: They're not interested in human rights.

EGGS: —on border issues particularly.

ANGELA: … Ali Ghozina, Branko Jenkiewicz, Maria Carbone, Maria Cricenti…

TOM: They're only interested in achieving phenomenal profits for people like themselves.

ANGELA: … Ulli Pangabeen, Kazuhiro Yamakaze…

EGGS: We are now the true radicals—

FI: You are now the caretakers of the future.

EGGS: —because we know that the individual is the only person who can take responsibility for his—*or her*—own life…

ANGELA: … Zevi Savvidis, Abdul Abdulla, and Sally Walker.

TOM: But keep the faith. Because there is a core of decency deep in the heart of every Australian—

EGGS: And we despise the predilection of the Left to run Australia down.

FI: So seize your future, girls. Make it your own.

TOM: So have a good one, all right!

EGGS: So here's to us! And God bless every one of you!

ANGELA: Give them all a round of applause, please!

Applause.

◆ ◆ ◆ ◆ ◆

SCENE TWO

Christmas at Warramee. Standing in the kitchen of their shared holiday home, the assembled family raise their glasses. They are wearing paper Christmas hats.

FI: Cheers, dears.

ALL: Happy Christmas.

FI: We're awfully glad you're here. It would have been a very sad little affair otherwise, wouldn't it Eggs? Just us.

EGGS: [*looking at the champagne label*] Barkers Hill? I didn't know they made champers. Yeah. Just the two of us. And Gramps.

ANGELA: Where is Gramps?

FI: He's having a little rest.

EGGS: Top up, Tom?

TOM: Not a bad drop.

EGGS: Feeble?

FI: Thanks, darling.

ANGELA: I thought Lockie had leave over Christmas?

FI: Not this year.

ANGELA: They're miserable bastards in the Navy, aren't they?

EGGS: Someone's got to defend the nation.

ANGELA: From boat people?

TOM: [*hastily*] Ange, do you want to check the turkey?

ANGELA: What?

TOM: The *turkey*.

FI: I think this oven's a bit dicky, actually.

EGGS: Dad had to have his groin photographed. Did he tell you?

TOM: No.

EGGS: This nurse comes in with a camera and tells him to drop his daks and Dad says, 'What's this all about?', and the nurse says, 'I'm making a porn film'. And Dad says, 'Well, it'll be soft porn'.

They laugh.

FI: Ssh. Ssh. You'll wake him.

TOM: He's refusing to go to Rehab, you know.

EGGS: Why?

TOM: Because it turns out the ambulance driver is a Japanese chappie.

FI: Well, that generation of men must find it very hard…

TOM: It's got nothing to do with it, Fi.

ANGELA: He won't get in a car driven by any brand of Asian.

TOM: They've got no peripheral vision, apparently.

EGGS *and* TOM *laugh. Eggs' mobile phone rings.*

EGGS: [*into the mobile*] Hello? Eggs Benedict. Yep. Yep.

FI: Lockie and I were very sad, Harry. We missed out on this darling little house in Walsh Street.

HARRY: I had a look at that place. My mate, Kosta Zikki, did the renos.

FI: Really? He's doing very well, isn't he?

>   HARRY *and* TOM *exchange glances.*

HARRY: Two bedrooms. Single front?

FI: That's it. It went for one point six.

TOM: That all?

EGGS: [*into the mobile*] Jesus!

HARRY: That's about right.

EGGS: [*into the mobile*] Right. Okay.

FI: A Chinese businessman bought it for his children. He lives in Beijing but the children are here at uni, so they need student digs. Isn't that criminal?

HARRY: Nah. You don't want to buy there. Not for an investment property. I've got something in mind for you two.

FI: Really?

HARRY: On the Esplanade. Roof garden. Looking out over the Elwood beach.

FI: Nice.

EGGS: [*into the mobile*] No. Absolutely not.

FI: How much?

HARRY: Under a mill, for sure. Needs a facelift…

FI: Of course.

EGGS: [*into the mobile*] No. Take no action. No action at all.

FI: Harry, can I ask you a planning question? Last week these workmen came and stuck these ghastly barbed-wire hoops right along the fence at the back of us in Camberwell.

EGGS: [*into the mobile*] No action. Got that? Just stand by. And keep me in the loop.

FI: So we look out from our breakfast nook at barbed-wire. Have we got any rights there? It looks like Baxter Detention Centre.

>   ANGELA *and* TOM *exchange glances.* HARRY *laughs, then stifles it.*

EGGS: [*into the mobile*] Okay. 'Bye. [*He hangs up.*] Sorry about that.

ANGELA: What was that all about?

EGGS: Oh, the usual. How's your bubbly?

ANGELA: Okay.

TOM: It's bloody hot in here, isn't it?

ANGELA: You were the one who insisted on turkey.

TOM: I was just thinking of Dad.

ANGELA: Bullshit.

HARRY: Yeah, last year we had seafood and you sulked.

TOM: I did not.

ANGELA: You did. Didn't he?

EGGS: I'm with Tom. All that smoked salmon and prawns and crap. Didn't feel like Christmas.

TOM: See?

EGGS: Too politically correct.

ANGELA: Jeez, you're a wanker.

EGGS: We want the roast bird, don't we Tommy?

TOM: Yep. Turkey, spuds, cranberry sauce.

EGGS: Followed by pud.

TOM: And brandy butter.

EGGS: And a snooze in the afternoon.

ANGELA: Typical.

> *The phone rings.*

FI: That'll be Lockie.

EGGS: [*into the phone*] Hello? Hello? Lachlan? Is that you? [*To the others*] It's Lockie calling from the ship.

FI: Is everything okay?

EGGS: Ssh. [*Into the phone*] Happy Christmas.

ALL: Happy Christmas, Lockie!

EGGS: [*into the phone*] What?! [*Pause.*] Just a minute. [*He moves down-stage out of earshot of the others.*] Look, this is not appropriate. This is totally out of line. I expect more of you, Lachlan. You should know better.

> *He walks back.* FI *is holding out her hand to speak.*

FI: Eggs?

EGGS: [*brightly into the phone*] Never mind. We'll see you in the New Year. Mum sends her love. Merry Christmas. [*He hangs up. To* FI] Sorry, darl. He couldn't talk.

FI: Ohh.

EGGS: They're in the middle of an operation.

FI: On Christmas Day?

TOM: No rest for the wicked.

FI *takes a moment to recover. The oven timer rings.*

ANGELA: What sort of operation would they do on Christmas Day?

HARRY: It won't be peace on earth, that's for sure.

FI: [*re the turkey*] I hope this is big enough. The little man at Jonathon's said four and a half kilos would do eight people.

ANGELA: Looks like a frigging emu.

On the verandah, EGGS *makes a quick call on his mobile.*

EGGS: [*into the mobile*] Get on to Jakarta. If you can't find anyone there who can speak English, send an email. And get them to confirm receipt of the email. Okay? See you.

EGGS *hangs up.* TOM *follows him out to the balcony.*

TOM: Everything okay with Lockie?

EGGS: Yeah. Good as gold. [*Beat.*] D'you ever feel like having another crack at the Sydney to Hobart?

TOM: Chug Masters is up there again this year.

EGGS: Lucky bastard. Would you do it again?

TOM: Like a shot.

EGGS: Me too. Remember when we were coming into Storm Bay?

TOM: Unbelievable. You're yelling at Chug, 'There's a front coming', and he's going, 'She'll be right. It's just a bullet.'

EGGS: I could see it. Clear as bloody day, you know.

TOM: If you hadn't seen that little tear in the mainsail on the luff…

EGGS: We would have gone, no question.

TOM: I thought we were gonna lose the mast.

EGGS: It was when you lost the sail overboard, that's when I thought it was all over, red rover.

TOM: Those waves must have been about fifteen foot. All I could think was cut the sheets. Cut the bloody sheets.

EGGS: The sail's wrapped around the rudder and the prop. No steerage, no prop! I'm about to cut it loose…

TOM: But ChuggyBoy's screaming, 'No, you bastard…'

TOM & EGGS: [*together*] 'That sail cost me three grand.'

TOM: Unbelievable. I tell you, when that sail flicked out from the starboard side, I thought, 'Chuggy, you lead a charmed life'.

EGGS: Did you? I thought, 'Chuggy, you bastard. That's the last time I'm gonna cover your arse.' [*Beat.*] But then, we won on handicap.

TOM *smiles.*

TOM: We did.

Silence. They both look out at the sea. TOM*'s mobile rings.*

Sorry. [*Into the mobile*] Tom Benedict. Merry Christmas to you too. Oh no. Oh, Jesus. Is he all right? Yeah. Okay. I'll come back to town later on. Yep. Yep. That's okay. Thanks, Duggie. Good man. See you.

He hangs up.

EGGS: Everything okay?

TOM: One of my Ethiopians. Just got hit by a car. He's got a broken pelvis and no Medicare rights. You can't keep this up. It's totally inhumane.

EGGS: Not today, Tom.

TOM: I'm taking this to the UN, if I can't get you to budge.

EGGS: Just hang on.

TOM: I went to the Review Tribunal three times to get that guy out of detention—

EGGS: Look, if you can just hold your horses, I'll tell you.

TOM: What?

EGGS: This is extremely sensitive.

TOM: Okay.

EGGS: The PM's going to retire at Easter.

TOM: I thought he'd bat till he dropped.

EGGS: It looks as if I've got the numbers.

TOM: What about the Treasurer?

EGGS: Yesterday's hero.

TOM: You sure?

EGGS: He's left his run too late.

TOM: Does he know you're a contender?

EGGS: Can't keep a thing like that quiet. The knives are out.

TOM: Jesus.

EGGS: The point is, if I am going to be Prime Minister, you're going to have to cool it.

TOM: Oh, c'mon, Eggs.

EGGS: No, wait! This is an opportunity for us both. Look, Tom, I can get you a plum job. United Nations, UNESCO, Human Rights Commission. London, New York, Geneva. You name it. You can do good, throughout the whole friggin' world, if you want. Just leave me Australia.

TOM: You're asking me to leave the country.

EGGS: I'm asking you to let me be PM.

TOM: You're trying to buy my silence.

EGGS: Tommy, you and I simply cannot go on playing out our disagreements on the national stage.

TOM: Why not? The Costellos manage it.

EGGS: Neither of us will survive.

TOM: Who else are you going to muzzle, Eggs? Is that what you want to stand for: political intimidation?

EGGS: Get off your high horse.

TOM: 'My government will not brook any dissent.'

EGGS: Look, you can sound off all you like to your leftie acolytes at bloody conferences. But I'm offering you real power. Without that, you're just pissing up against the wall.

TOM: There was a time when you found debate healthy.

EGGS: Tom, I intend to run the country. And I will not be shot in the foot at every turn, by my own brother.

> *Later.* ANGELA *is in the kitchen.* TOM *enters.*

TOM: Eggs wants us to re-locate. Overseas.

ANGELA: Oh, for Chrissake.

TOM: Or I could just shut up.

ANGELA: He actually tried to bully you into leaving Australia?

TOM: No, not bully. [*Beat.*] Bribe.

ANGELA: He's scared.

TOM: He reckons he's got a crack at the top job.

ANGELA: He's well qualified—he doesn't believe in anything.

TOM: Yes he does.

ANGELA: 'How can I make life more cushy for the silvertails?'

TOM: I have to go to Melbourne.

ANGELA: Oh, no. Not tonight.

TOM: Sorry.

ANGELA: It's Christmas.

> *Later that night,* EGGS *enters to find* FI *sitting alone listening to the Kings College Cambridge Choir singing 'I Saw Three Ships Came Sailing By'.* FI *puts her arms around his neck. They kiss.*

FI: Have you had a nice day?

EGGS: Top turkey.

FI: It was good, wasn't it? What was all that about with Lockie?

EGGS: A boat's gone down.

FI: A Navy boat?

EGGS: An Indonesian fishing boat. Packed to the gunnels with asylum
   seekers.

FI: Oh, how frightful. Is Lockie involved?

EGGS: No.

FI: But he knows about it?

EGGS: Mm-hmm.

FI: So he is involved?

EGGS: Lockie is perfectly safe, so don't get yourself worked up.

FI: Why wouldn't you let him speak to me?

EGGS: It just wasn't possible, Fi. [*Beat.*] I have to go to Melbourne.

FI: Oh, no. Not tonight.

EGGS: Sorry.

FI: You promised me you'd make time to talk to Tom.

EGGS: I have.

FI: About Marty?

EGGS: Oh. No.

FI: 'Course not. [*Beat.*] Who was that on the phone?

EGGS: The office.

FI: Jamie.

◆ ◆ ◆ ◆ ◆

SCENE THREE

Eggs' office. EGGS *and* JAMIE *watch videos of last night's news.*

INTERVIEWER: [*voice-over from the television*] But first, one man's
   shocking ordeal. We thought the flood of asylum seekers was over.
   But now—the tragedy of the *Kelepasan*—the Indonesian fishing
   boat which sank in the Indian Ocean, on Christmas Day. This morning,
   the sole survivor Hazem Al Ayad returned to Melbourne. With him—
   refugee advocate Tom Benedict, Director of the Lawson Foundation.

TOM: [*voice-over from the television*] This was a full-scale emergency
   but the government failed to launch a rescue operation. And why?

Because this government is not concerned with saving the lives of innocent people. They are engaged in the most disgraceful and immoral activity they've ever undertaken—to make sure that these desperate and destitute people do not set foot on our soil.

EGGS: Bloody Tom. What's he playing at?

JAMIE: I thought you told him to pull his head in.

EGGS: I did.

JAMIE: He's a pain in the arse. That was on Seven, Nine and Ten—prime-time news in all mainland capitals.

EGGS: What kind of coverage did I get?

JAMIE: ABC Perth and six o'clock Tassie.

EGGS: Shit.

JAMIE: If there's a problem it'll be the Iraqi guy. The survivor. Look at this.

> JAMIE *hits the remote.*

HAZEM: [*voice-over from the television*] The boat sink very quick. I cannot find my family in the water. I hold on to plank of wood for twenty hour. Everywhere I put my arm, a drowned child or woman bobs up and lift my arm. I see dead children like birds floating on the water.

EGGS: Great. Just what we need.

JAMIE: A Muslim who understands the five-second grab.

EGGS: Jesus, Jamie.

JAMIE: Well, he's not some freak who's sewn up his lips.

EGGS: He's our problem. You're right.

JAMIE: Only if the punters get to know him.

EGGS: Tom's onto it, of course. Straight away. Quick as you can say Jack Robinson, he's touting him around. Getting the bleeding hearts thumping away.

> JAMIE *hands* EGGS *a folder.*

JAMIE: I've dug out his file. He was in Baxter for three years, then on a temporary protection visa for twelve months.

EGGS: Right.

JAMIE: And then his wife decided to come with their two daughters. So he flew to Indonesia to come back with her on the boat.

EGGS: The *Kelepasan.*

JAMIE: Yep.

EGGS: Jesus, what a mess.

The intercom buzzes.

JAMIE: Yeah?

ERIC: [*voice-over on the intercom*] The childcare centre's on the phone.

JAMIE: I'm not here.

ERIC: [*voice-over on the intercom*] Your daughter's sick.

JAMIE: I told you. I'm not here.

EGGS: He'll probably want special consideration for his visa.

JAMIE: He forfeited his visa when he left the country.

EGGS: There'll be a huge outcry, you know, if I knock him back.

JAMIE: Mate, we deported the Bakhtiyaris on Boxing Day.

Jamie's mobile rings.

[*Into the mobile*] Jamie Savage. [*Pause.*] Bloody hell. [*Pause.*] Listen, mate. Your fault. You fix it. Next time tell your boss to shut his trap.

She hangs up.

EGGS: Who was that?

JAMIE: Bob Fuller's minder. The Honourable Member has just been on his local radio station—

EGGS: Oh, not again.

JAMIE: A listener rang in and said there was something dodgy about the sinking of the *Kelepasan*.

EGGS: And Bob agreed? Oh, Christ.

JAMIE: He's a bloody sook.

EGGS: He's a bloody catastrophe.

JAMIE: What if he starts asking questions?

EGGS: Then we start asking about all those young boys working on his electoral campaign.

JAMIE: Good.

EGGS *exits.* JAMIE *punches numbers into her phone.*

[*Into the phone*] Geoff? Jamie. Just been talking to Bob Fuller's office. On no account is he to have access to the Coastwatch documents. Got that? If the media pick this up—shovel it back onto the Indonesians. Nothing to do with us.

◆ ◆ ◆ ◆ ◆

SCENE FOUR

HAZEM *and* TOM *sit at the kitchen table.* ANGELA *pours* HAZEM *a cup of tea. Beat.*

TOM: It's going to be a long hard slog, matey.

HAZEM: The man who is an optimist... is a fool.

ANGELA: At least we can give thanks that you're here.

TOM: And safe.

HAZEM: God spared me for a reason. But every day and every night I search for that reason. In my heart I believe I should not live. When I see my daughter floating dead, I say to God, 'This is because of me'.

TOM: Perhaps God spared you, so you could tell the world what happened.

HAZEM: I did this. I bring my family to their death.

ANGELA: Fatima was determined to come. There was nothing you could do.

From left: Nicholas Eadie as Tom, Rodney Afif as Hazem and Laura Lattuada as Angela in the 2005 STC / MTC production. (Photo: Jeff Busby)

TOM: You tried, remember?

HAZEM: When I escaped from Iraq—my brother Mohammed was killed. So I took my family to Iran. But they do not let my children into school. They do not let me rent property. Official order. No rent to foreigners. No employ Afghanis or Iraqis. You are educated people. You can see. What choice did I have?

TOM: [*together*] Of course.

ANGELA: [*together*] Mmm.

HAZEM: Fatima, she say to me, 'If we go back to Iraq, one hundred per cent chance, we die. If we come to Australia, ninety per cent chance…' When I was in the water that night I saw a woman in the dark. I cry out to her. I say, 'My family, all drown. I want to die.' She turn around. I see is my wife Fatima. I praise God. I say, 'Thank you merciful God'. Fatima, she cling to wood with me. Hour after hour. Then she get weak. From petrol in the water. She cannot stop crying for her daughters. She say she want to die. I hold her. But I swallow too much water. I choke. Then she say, 'Forgive me'. And she let go of wood.

He weeps.

TOM: Oh, mate. This is really tough.

Beat.

HAZEM: Do you believe in evil?

TOM: Evil?

HAZEM: You never look into a man's eyes and thought there is evil?

TOM: I'm not sure, I…

HAZEM: When I think that I am unwelcome in every country on this earth, when I think that people in this country want my family to drown, rather than step foot on this shore, then I find it hard not to believe in evil. What have the little children done? Nothing. What has my wife done? My wife—one year and one month waiting for reply from United Nations. Waiting. Waiting. Waiting.

◆ ◆ ◆ ◆ ◆

SCENE FIVE

In the therapist's office.

THERAPIST: Sorry to keep you waiting.

FI: It's fine.

EGGS: One of the features of my job is that you never wait. You can't miss an important Cabinet meeting simply because you had to wait—

FI: Because it'd be wrong for my husband to miss a high-level meeting because he'd had spent his ministerial time waiting in a waiting room.

THERAPIST: I'm sorry. Sometimes it gets like that here.

FI: He doesn't even dial his own phone, you know, Pam. He has a man to do that for him.

> *Beat.*

THERAPIST: So how can I help you?

EGGS: Fi's the one who wanted to come. Apparently I've become a callous bastard.

THERAPIST: Uh-huh. Is that how you see it?

EGGS: Sure.

THERAPIST: Does it concern you?

EGGS: It's not why I'm here.

THERAPIST: Why are you here?

> *Beat.*

EGGS: My son died of a drug overdose.

THERAPIST: How long ago was that?

FI: Two and a half years.

THERAPIST: Did you seek any professional help at the time? Grief counselling?

FI: My husband had an election to win.

THERAPIST: What was your boy's name?

FI: [*together*] Marty.

EGGS: [*together*] Martin.

THERAPIST: Did you know that Marty used drugs?

EGGS: Why do you ask that?

THERAPIST: Some parents don't know.

EGGS: Some inattentive ones?

> *Silence.*

My brother knew. Marty told him everything.

THERAPIST: Why was that?

EGGS: Tom's in the same game as you. The compassion industry.

FI: Tom had Marty's trust.

EGGS: I tried to talk to Marty. I tried everything.

FI: No you didn't.

EGGS: I bloody well did. You don't know the half of it.

FI: Which half is that?

EGGS: You were the boy's mother. Where were you?

> *Pause.*

FI: These kids have too much money. They've got cars and ipods. Whatever they want. Fifty dollars for a little pill. It's nothing. He was only seventeen.

EGGS: Martin had no capacity for self discipline. And I could have helped him. Because I'm not afraid of being tough. But Tom. He knew better. Of course. He thinks being a parent is just about being matey.

FI: But at least he has a relationship with his boy.

EGGS: I had a relationship with Marty. It just wasn't the kind of relationship you wanted me to have. Wallowing in feelings. You see what the problem is, Pam. She didn't want Marty to be a man.

FI: I just feel if we could forgive each other…

EGGS: See, I don't believe that for a minute. My wife is a very good woman. She's a beautiful woman. She's depressed. Understandably. But she has this Christian idea that forgiveness is the panacea for everything. Forgiveness is crap. It's just a form of moral repression. It's about burying rage and blame. Which we have a right to feel.

THERAPIST: What do you think, Fi?

FI: I feel rage and blame all the time. But it doesn't seem to be helping.

EGGS: You don't let yourself feel rage. Rage is one of the great forces of life.

FI: You see it all the time, don't you? Politicians' kids going off the rails.

EGGS: Stop. Stop. Just stop right there! No one is to blame here, except Martin. He went to a party. His choice. He took drugs. His choice. He knew the risks. Every step of the way. His choice. Marty's choice. Marty's choice. Marty's choice. And will you stop comparing me to my brother? It's driving me crazy. My brother is a stubborn mule. Completely incapable of compromise. The moral certitude is staggering. My brother puts family before politics. And this makes him a great man in my wife's eyes. But I can't do that. That's my choice. I came here today. My choice. And now I'm leaving. You do what you want.

> *He exits.*

FI: Thank you for trying.

SCENE SIX (A)

Warramee at Easter. The family has gathered for Fi's birthday. They all sing 'Happy Birthday' then raise their champagne glasses.

FI: Cheers, dears!
ALL: Cheers!
LACHLAN: Happy birthday, Mum!
ANGELA: And welcome home, Lockie!
ALL: Yes! / Welcome!
LACHLAN: Thanks.

> TOM *presents a large heavy present.*

TOM: Happy birthday, Fi.
FI: Ooh, thank you. Look at this. What is it, ever?
ANGELA: Open it and find out.
TOM: [*holding up his glass*] This is very nice, isn't it?
EGGS: Barkers Hill. We had it at Christmas.

> FI *unwraps the huge vase that was broken in the Prologue.*

FI: Oh, isn't that lovely? Very Mediterranean. So unusual. Where did you get it?
TOM: Victoria Market.
FI: Goodness. You can find such unusual things there, can't you? Let's see. I think I might like to keep it down here. [*To* EGGS] What do you think, darling? It wouldn't really go at our place.
EGGS: I hear they've asked you to give the Valedictory Speech at Grammar this year?
TOM: What d'you mean, 'You hear'? You're on the Board.
EGGS: I was in Canberra.

ANGELA: He would've voted against it.

EGGS: Not at all. My brother has exactly the kind of principled outlook we want in our future leaders. Although you did get expelled.

LACHLAN: Serious?

TOM: Suspended.

LACHLAN: What a legend.

TOM: I walked over to the Shrine one lunchtime and tried to toast my sandwiches on the eternal flame. So they suspended me.

EGGS: He was just a nerdy little Christian before that.

TOM: My best mate Chug Masters told everyone that it was an anti-war statement. Suddenly I was the school radical.

EGGS: Which is how you cracked onto Mandy McMillan—the Merton Hall Marxist.

TOM: She tongue-kissed me at the tennis club social.

HARRY: Too much information, Dad.

TOM: She was a great pash, Mandy McMillan.

From left: Garry McDonald as Eggs, Ben Lawson as Lachlan, Hamish Michael as Harry, Laura Lattuada as Angela and Nicholas Eadie as Tom in the 2005 STC / MTC production. (Photo: Jeff Busby)

EGGS: I'll say.

ANGELA: Honestly. You two.

FI: Boys, would you check the meat?

TOM: Her old man was the first person I'd ever met who voted for the ALP.

HARRY: You're joking?

TOM: The Labor Party had never been in government in our lifetime, had they?

EGGS: No. They were the great days. More bubbles, Ange?

ANGELA: No.

TOM: I assumed that was how democracy worked. The Liberal Party ruled and the vulgar Labor Party protested about things—and asked questions.

> *The boys exit.*

ANGELA: But you wouldn't expect them to actually govern. To do that, you had to go to Grammar and play in the First Eleven.

EGGS: As it should be.

ANGELA: As it is.

SCENE SIX (B)

HARRY *and* LACHLAN *are prodding the kettle barbeque.*

HARRY: Do you get a cabin to yourself on the ship, being a Lieutenant Commander?

LACHLAN: I'm a Gunnery Officer. And Assistant PWO [*pee-woh*].

HARRY: What's that?

LACHLAN: A PWO? Principal Warfare Officer.

HARRY: There's a job title.

LACHLAN: It's great. Never been happier. You know, the best thing about the Navy is your mates. I could name twenty blokes who are close friends. You make decent money. And next year they're gonna pay for me to do a degree in oceanography.

> *They take the lid off the barbeque.*

HARRY: Is this cooked?

LACHLAN: How do you tell?

HARRY: Fucked if I know.

Beat. EGGS *bangs on the glass: 'Put the lid on—you're letting the heat out.'*

LACHLAN: Hey, I read in the paper that there's this new drug—9/11. Sounds pretty full on.

HARRY: Fuckin' hell.

LACHLAN: Have you tried it?

HARRY: I don't do drugs anymore.

LACHLAN: Someone told me you and Marty shared the tab of E, that night. Half each. [*Beat.*] Look mate, I'm not pointing the finger. I'm a big believer in personal responsibility.

Beat.

HARRY: What do your Navy mates think about personal responsibility? When they're towing those boats out to sea.

LACHLAN: We have to stop them coming, Harry. There's tens of thousands of them. It's all starting up again.

HARRY: But where else can they go?

LACHLAN: Not here. They're not our responsibility.

HARRY: Why not?

LACHLAN: Because they don't fit in. And before you know it, everything that's good about this country is up shit creek.

HARRY: But that's bullshit. You've swallowed it hook, line and sinker, mate. All the party propaganda. At least have the guts to—

LACHLAN: You think you'd be different, don't you? Well, let me tell you. You don't know unless you're tested. But you were tested once. I know this about you, Harry. The night Marty died. And you didn't even go with him in the ambulance to the hospital.

HARRY: Mate, I wasn't in possession of my faculties.

LACHLAN: No. Still. It was gutless. Wasn't it? See, I know about this, because I am tested every day. And every day I know what a struggle it is to step up to the mark. What happened to Marty…

HARRY: Could've happened to anyone.

LACHLAN: Maybe. But at the end of the day there was always something weak about my brother.

SCENE SIX (C)

EGGS *moves to* TOM.

EGGS: Have you thought about my proposal?
TOM: What proposal?
EGGS: At Christmas.
TOM: Your bribe, you mean?
EGGS: There's a job going in Brussels. At the Global Crisis Centre.
TOM: I'm not interested.
EGGS: Ange is not interested, you mean.
TOM: I like my job at the Lawson Foundation.
EGGS: What do you earn? Peanuts, I bet.
TOM: None of your business.
EGGS: Eighty? Ninety?
TOM: Sixty.
EGGS: Sixty? [*He laughs.*] Oh, mate.

      ANGELA *and* FI *enter.*

ANGELA: I'm really glad you've agreed to do this, Fi.
EGGS: What has she agreed to do?
FI: The Lawson Foundation has set up a new housing program for heroin users.
TOM: Fi's gonna be our patron.
FI: You told me to get involved in a cause.
EGGS: Have you run that past Jamie?
FI: Why?
EGGS: For the same reason that everything goes through Jamie. You don't want to be seen doing something that contravenes government policy.
FI: I trust that helping heroin addicts does not contravene government policy.

      Beat.

ANGELA: Lockie! Harry! How's the barbie going?
EGGS: So what's Harry up to? Bit of a loose end, by the looks of it.
ANGELA: He's tendering for a whole lot of jobs.

TOM: But you're right, he hasn't got work.

ANGELA: That's work.

TOM: It's not a paying job. And given that he's Mr Lifestyle...

FI: They're all like that.

EGGS: Lachlan isn't. He's a real Benedict. You're very hard on our old man, Tommy, but what Dad gave us was a strong sense of public service.

ANGELA: He gave you both egos the size of Mount Olympus.

>   FI *giggles.*

EGGS: It's called self esteem. You'll find most people who make a contribution have a healthy dose of it.

TOM: Harry hasn't got a self esteem problem.

EGGS: No, but he's not a leader. That's the difference between a Grammar education and a high school.

TOM & ANGELA: [*together*] Oh, here we go.

EGGS: You're so down on it, Tom, but you've got Grammar to thank for making you the man you are. As has Lachlan.

ANGELA: He's in the military, for Chrissake.

EGGS: This is precisely the reason why the Left is so ineffectual.

FI: Eggs!

EGGS: Your refusal to think about defence issues.

FI: Eggs!

TOM: And the Prime Minister was *thinking* when he decided to invade Iraq?

EGGS: The Prime Minister took a principled stand.

FI: Eggs.

EGGS: More than you can say for your lot.

TOM: Oh, please. The Prime Minister was conned by American fundamentalists—

FI: Enough, please, both of you.

TOM: Sorry.

EGGS: Okay.

ANGELA: Harry is a young architect working in a very competitive climate.

EGGS: He tarts up other people's kitchens, for God's sake.

ANGELA: You want him to design battleships?

EGGS: I want him to be a bloody architect! A man with the courage to take hold of the built environment and reshape it.

TOM: Everyone makes their mark in different ways, Eggs.

EGGS: Your son isn't driving his own life. He lolls about hoping for someone else to give him a job.

ANGELA: Well, that's how life is—out here in the real world, Minister.

EGGS: Exactly! But at Grammar you learn to take control. No one ever taught us how to 'write a résumé', Angela. Or how to do job interviews. And you know why? Because they knew we'd be conducting them.

TOM: What Harry has in spades—is empathy. He's completely comfortable with people from all different walks of life. We didn't even learn how to talk to women.

EGGS: We did all right.

ANGELA: Harry is thoughtful and kind and creative.

EGGS: And frightened of being a man.

TOM: Bullshit. You have some 1950s idea of what manliness is supposed to be.

EGGS: Look, all I'm saying is that I can't bear this suburban crap that says, 'Don't get ideas above your station'.

ANGELA: Your father got ideas above his station and look what happened to him.

TOM: Ange?

EGGS: What?

ANGELA: He went bankrupt.

EGGS: So?

ANGELA: It destroyed your family.

EGGS: It did not.

TOM: Oh, come off it, Eggs. Of course it did.

ANGELA: Your mother died.

EGGS: And we were stronger because of it.

FI: It was the defining moment in your life.

EGGS: Of course it was. Our father's construction company was nobbled by the unions. Greedy, lazy bastards. Made it impossible for people with vision to make a difference.

TOM: Our father was ripping off an immigrant workforce and when he was called to account, the whole bloody edifice crumbled, taking our mother with it.

EGGS: It showed me the terrible threat of mob rule.

TOM: It taught me that there's more to life than being rich.

The boys enter with a platter of barbequed lamb.

LACHLAN: Grub's up.

TOM: Ooh, that looks good.

FI: Thanks, darling. Over here.

EGGS: So, how's it going, Harry?

HARRY: Okay.

EGGS: You got a squeeze?

HARRY: Sorry?

EGGS: A squeeze.

LACHLAN: A girlfriend.

HARRY: Squeeze? No.

EGGS: Good-looking bloke like you. Thought you would have been chasing them away.

HARRY: I have. Beating them off.

EGGS: Just biding your time, are you? Playing the field?

Beat.

HARRY: Help.

EGGS: Like Lockie here. He's a sly dog. What happened to that girl you were going out with? The dumpy one? Gretel.

LACHLAN: Tabitha.

EGGS: Yeah. Her.

HARRY: Too dumpy.

LACHLAN: Shut up.

EGGS: Come on, Lock.

HARRY: She was a big girl.

EGGS: Face facts.

FI: She had a pretty face.

LACHLAN: Do you mind?

TOM: Australia and Pakistan at the G on Friday night, Lock. Wanna come?

LACHLAN: Shit yeah.

TOM: What about if I meet you at the Duke. We'll have a few beers first.

LACHLAN: Sweet.

EGGS: I thought we were having dinner together. At the Club?

LACHLAN: Oh, yeah. Yeah. I forgot.

FI: Why don't you all go to the cricket?

EGGS: Because I've booked at the Club.

SCENE SIX (D)

Later that night, on the balcony, EGGS, FI *and* LACHLAN *debrief.*

EGGS: What was that yellow stuff on the brussel sprouts?

LACHLAN: Peanut butter.

EGGS: I think I've got an upset stomach.

FI: It was chestnut puree.

EGGS: Why did my brother marry that woman?

LACHLAN: She's sexy.

EGGS: You find crassness sexy?

LACHLAN: Must do.

> LACHLAN *exits.*

FI: I tried very hard today.

EGGS: I know. Thank you.

FI: Do you think they know it's all a charade?

EGGS: Please, Fi.

FI: I know they're laughing at us.

EGGS: Why would they be doing that?

FI: Because we're ridiculous.

EGGS: I must say I didn't go for that peanut butter stuff.

FI: When we're with them, it's like we become ridiculous parodies of ourselves. They make us ridiculous.

EGGS: I don't know what you're talking about.

FI: You become a completely pompous ass. And I become a sort of dippy South Yarra blonde.

EGGS: I don't think I'm pompous.

> EGGS *wanders off.*

SCENE SIX (E)

TOM, ANGELA *and* HARRY *clean up the kitchen. They whisper.*

ANGELA: Does anybody else feel the need to have a bath—just to wash off the stench of power?

TOM: What was that yellow stuff on the brussel sprouts?

HARRY: Chestnut purée.

ANGELA: Excuse me?

HARRY: Yaya makes it, you freak.

ANGELA: My mother makes *skordalia me kastana*.

HARRY: Same thing.

ANGELA: It is not. It is nothing like that chestnut sauce that Fi made.

HARRY: Jeez, she hates it when Anglos do wog stuff better than the wogs.

TOM: I'll say.

HARRY: What about when Fi made that *melitzanes moussaka*?

ANGELA: It was horrible.

HARRY: It was not.

ANGELA: She used Kraft cheese.

TOM: How un-fucking-called-for.

ANGELA: It was so… *Women's Weekly*.

HARRY: I rest my case.

> HARRY *exits.*

ANGELA: I don't know why I get so thingy. It's because they run everything anyway and you just think, 'Bugger off. At least leave me my
own cooking.'

> *Tom's mobile rings.*

TOM: [*into the mobile*] Tom Benedict. Hey, Pablo, how's it going?
You're kidding. Yes. Yes. Yes. You are a brilliant and beautiful man
and I love you. Hang on, I'll just tell Ange. [*To* ANGELA] We've just
won permanent visas for six more Afghanis.

ANGELA: Including Nafeesah?

TOM: [*nodding excitedly*] Yes, Nafeesah. Oh, brilliant. Brilliant. [*Into
the mobile*] Hey, Pablo. How's Hazem? How's his spirits?

ANGELA: Ask him to come over on the weekend.

TOM: [*into the mobile*] Right. Okay. Oh no. Has he got someone there
with him? I'll call him tomorrow. Thanks, mate. Cheers.

> *He hangs up.*

ANGELA: How is he?

TOM: Hazem? Depressed.

ANGELA: Hardly surprising. How long before he finds out whether they'll
give him a visa?

TOM: Could be months.

ANGELA: And all the time he's got the worry, hanging over his head. Am I gonna be able to stay or am I gonna get deported.

TOM: I'm doing my best, Ange.

ANGELA: No you're not.

TOM: I bloody well am.

ANGELA: You're faffing around with the Immigration Department.

TOM: I am lobbying the media as hard as I can.

ANGELA: But why aren't you lobbying *him*? Go and talk to him.

TOM: No. I don't want to bring political issues into the family. Not here.

ANGELA: Why not? He would. He's the Minister twenty-four hours a day.

TOM: No. Once you start to do that—

ANGELA: What?

TOM: Well, I don't work like that.

ANGELA: And so Hazem gets deported. But what's that matter? So long as you uphold the good old Benedict code.

TOM: This is not the place. He won't engage with it here.

ANGELA: He's an arsehole.

TOM: Tell me something I don't know.

ANGELA: You have to be an arsehole too.

TOM: I have to be a strategic arsehole.

SCENE SIX (F)

EGGS *is examining the barbeque with* LACHLAN *and* HARRY.

EGGS: See, strictly speaking, your kettle barbie's different to your grill. You're using your indirect cooking here. And using woodsmoke as a flavouring agent. You're not just chucking your meat on the open flame and burning it to buggery. I hate that thing Tom uses. Makes the meat taste like the inside of a Zippo lighter. See this is good, this porcelain enamelled lid. It gives you your rust protection. It's got a very low iron content which makes it more resistant.

    EGGS *exits.*

HARRY: No wonder you joined the Navy. Your old man's a freak.

LACHLAN: I know. He's getting worse.

HARRY: I liked him better when he was Veterans' Affairs.

LACHLAN *slaps a mozzie on his leg.*

You know how he was bullying you about getting a share portfolio?

LACHLAN: He wasn't bullying.

HARRY: He was. If he was my old man, I'd tell him to pull his head in.

LACHLAN: I thought it was a good idea.

HARRY: Oh, you are such a suck.

LACHLAN: You have to think about retirement.

HARRY: You're twenty-four, Lockie. That's just sick.

LACHLAN: You and I think differently.

HARRY: You don't think. Full stop. You just do what your old man says.

LACHLAN: Fuck off.

HARRY: Just don't be too gullible, PWO.

LACHLAN: Oh, man, that's rich. It kills me the way you think you know it all. But you know nothing.

HARRY: I know they're turning you into a Nazi.

LACHLAN: That's right, you've been on a ship when they've sloshed the deck with petrol and set it on fire? You've seen them brawling? Look at this.

He shows his arm

HARRY: Shit. Is that a bite mark?

LACHLAN: This [*the bite*] is my souvenir from the *Burung*—last October. This woman was hiding in the wheelhouse. She leapt out and bit me. And then she hung on until I was spurting blood.

HARRY: Why did she do that?

LACHLAN: Because she was a nutter.

HARRY: She was probably terrified.

LACHLAN: Well, they brought it on themselves. We did everything we could to get that boat to turn around. We sent them warnings in English and Bahasa. All the usual stuff. No response. We even pounded them with twenty-three rounds in the water. Nothing. So we had to take the boat by force.

HARRY: With guns and stuff?

LACHLAN: It was a madhouse on that boat. All the SUNCs were crying and screaming; running from side to side.

HARRY: SUNCs?

LACHLAN: Suspected unlawful non-citizens.

HARRY: Bloody hell.

LACHLAN: Yeah, yeah. It's just what everyone calls them. Kids are vomiting. They've got gastro. We're using intravenous drips to rehydrate them. And all the while I'm in the wheelhouse, steering them back out to sea.

HARRY: Jesus, Lock.

LACHLAN: Then the engine just dies on me. It's like it can't face the voyage back. And I've got waves crashing over the bows. Three minutes later—the boat starts to sink. And the SUNCs are jumping into the water. Everywhere you looked there were just heads bobbing about in the swell. It took three hours, Harry. Sailors dived in after them. We saved two hundred people. We were fucking heroes out there. Not that anyone gives a shit. We risked our lives. And yet we're the ones copping all the flack. You go around telling everyone we're Nazis. But that's not how the Navy operates. Canberra maybe. But not the Navy.

◆ ◆ ◆ ◆ ◆

SCENE SEVEN

ANGELA *is in the kitchen at her home.* HARRY *enters.*

HARRY: What's for tea?

ANGELA: Chops.

HARRY: Shit. I asked Lockie to come for dinner.

ANGELA: Great.

HARRY: He thinks we're proper Greeks.

ANGELA: We are.

HARRY: He thinks we eat dips.

ANGELA: We're chop-eating Greeks. From the south. [*Beat.*] How come you're so chummy with him all of a sudden?

He ushers her to the window.

HARRY: Feast your eyes on that piece of exquisite design.

ANGELA: What is it? A hang-glider.

HARRY: Beautiful, eh?

ANGELA: Oh, Harry, you haven't bought it?

HARRY: Lockie and me. Half each.

ANGELA: [*Greek*] *Ah re!* [Oh you!] How much?

HARRY: Four grand.

ANGELA: [*Greek*] *Porsa leftah!* [How much money?] Where are you getting all this money? New skis last month. The suit for Evdokea's wedding. The mountain bike.

HARRY: Haven't you heard of plastic?

ANGELA: [*Greek*] *Ah themoo! Themoo! Themoo!* [Omiod! Omigod! Omigod!]

HARRY: Anyway, I hear about the tender on Friday.

ANGELA: And what happens if you don't get it? Huh?

HARRY: Thanks, Mum. Thanks for the confidence.

ANGELA: Honestly, Harry.

HARRY: Mothers are supposed to say, 'You can move mountains'.

ANGELA: Just don't tell your father.

TOM *enters.*

TOM: Hey, HarryBoy. How's it going?

ANGELA: He just spent four thousand dollars on a hang-glider.

TOM: Jesus wept.

HARRY: Two thousand actually.

TOM: Hang-gliding? That's really gonna muss your hair.

HARRY: Funny, Dad.

TOM: I thought you were short of dough.

HARRY: Look. Chill out, will you? Most people live happy and fulfilled lives on credit.

Beat.

ANGELA: Did you get tomato sauce?

TOM: [*putting sauce on the table*] What's for tea?

ANGELA: *Paithakia ala hasapika.*

TOM: What's that?

HARRY: Chops.

TOM: Great. I asked Hazem for dinner. He's crazy about chops.

There is a knock at the door. We hear a voice off:

LACHLAN: [*offstage*] Yoo hoo?

LACHLAN *enters.*

TOM: Hey, Lockie. Good to see you.

LACHLAN: Hey, Tom. Auntie Ange.

He hugs ANGELA.

ANGELA: Lockie. Darling. Look at you! Ah! How can you bear being so handsome.

LACHLAN *laughs good-naturedly.*

HARRY: Sorry. She gets weirder by the day. Wanna beer?

LACHLAN: Cool.

TOM: You can try my home brew. It's good this time around. See, most home brewers keep their brew too warm during fermentation— usually around twenty-six degrees, but this time I kept it around twenty-one degrees and it's really avoided that cidery taste it gets.

LACHLAN: Okay.

TOM: [*watching him take a sip*] What d'you reckon?

LACHLAN *makes a face.*

LACHLAN: Ah. Good.

TOM: Good man. No chemicals. That's the secret.

LACHLAN: Right. What do you think of our new toy out there?

TOM & ANGELA: [*together*] Great.

HARRY *is incredulous.*

TOM: So how's everything at home, Lock?

LACHLAN: [*rolling his eyes*] I've been back two seconds, right? And already Dad's got me varnishing the deck.

TOM: Are you listening to this, HarryBoy?

HARRY: No.

The doorbell rings.

TOM: That'll be Hazem. I'll get it.

TOM *exits.*

LACHLAN: I tell you, this morning he's going, 'No, not like that. Do it like this.' I had to stop myself from pushing him off.

ANGELA: So everything's normal.

HAZEM *enters.*

HARRY: *Hazamm!*

ANGELA: Hazem! Hi.

HAZEM: Hello, Ange. Harry.

HARRY: This is my cousin Lachlan.

HAZEM: Hello.

They shake hands.

LACHLAN: *Boos teezi.*

HAZEM: Pardon?

LACHLAN: *Boos teezi.*

HAZEM: Excuse me?

LACHLAN: It means 'Hello' in Arabic. This Iraqi guy taught me.

HAZEM: *Boos teezi?*

LACHLAN: Yeah.

HARRY: What's it mean?

HAZEM: Kiss my arse.

They laugh.

LACHLAN: Bastard.

HARRY: Good one, Lock. Hey, Hazam. Want a beer?

HAZEM: Thank you.

HARRY: You can have one of Dad's. Or you can have a Coopers.

HAZEM: You make this beer yourself?

TOM: Mm-hmm. In the garage.

HAZEM: I try Tom's.

HARRY: You sure?

HAZEM: No worries. Cheers!

TOM: Cheers! What d'you reckon?

HAZEM: Ah? [*He makes a face.*] Good.

TOM: Good man. No chemicals. That's the secret. So, how's the taxi driving?

HAZEM: You know who I drive four o'clock this morning?

TOM: Who?

HAZEM: Rod Stewart.

TOM: Bullshit.

HAZEM: Is true. I drive and I look in mirror and I think: I know this man. Is Rod Stewart. No worries.

ANGELA: Oh, I've got a real soft spot for Rod Stewart.

HARRY: See what I mean? Beyond help!

TOM: Now what do you reckon, Hazem? [*Re the beer*] I want your honest opinion.

HAZEM: [*grinning, he takes another sip.*] Maybe you could get chemical.

They laugh.

LACHLAN: What did you do in Iraq?

HAZEM: Geography teacher. Before the uprising. You been there?

LACHLAN: No.

ANGELA: Lockie's in the Navy.

HAZEM: Ah.

ANGELA: So he's met quite a few Iraqis, lately. In leaky boats.

LACHLAN: I don't agree with this, Ange. But I don't have a choice.

ANGELA: That's bullshit. You do. You do have a choice.

TOM: Ange.

HARRY: Mum, give it a rest.

ANGELA: What? Well, he does have a choice. I'm sorry, Lockie. You know I love you. I just have a problem with the military.

TOM: Hazem was on the *Kelepasan.*

LACHLAN: Shit.

HAZEM: You know this boat?

LACHLAN: I've heard of it.

HARRY: Hazem was the only survivor.

HAZEM: You know something. After the boat capsize, I see three ships. I think: they come to rescue. But none of them come close. The people say one is Australia Navy.

LACHLAN: No. It wasn't.

TOM: Hazem. Did you just say that an Australian Navy boat was there.

HAZEM: Yes. I see it.

LACHLAN: No there wasn't.

ANGELA: How do you know?

LACHLAN: I just know. No Navy ship would stand by with people in the water. It just wouldn't happen.

TOM: Why didn't you tell me this?

HAZEM: The people in Indonesia say, 'No make trouble'. You say this about Navy boat and you no get visa.

ANGELA: That's outrageous.

HAZEM: They say, the government gave order not to rescue.

LACHLAN: No. Absolutely not. Who's they?

HAZEM: Pardon me?

LACHLAN: Who said the government gave the order?

HAZEM: The fishing boat that rescue me in the morning.

LACHLAN: No. That's wrong.

TOM: What do you know about this, Lachlan?

LACHLAN: Just what I read in the paper.

ANGELA: Hazem was there, Lockie. He saw an Australian Navy ship. He saw it with his own eyes.

◆ ◆ ◆ ◆ ◆

SCENE EIGHT

LACHLAN *and* FI. FI *is cleaning out her cupboards to give clothing to the Lawson Foundation.*

FI: [*holding up a cocktail dress*] Is this too good for the poor?

LACHLAN: They sell them, don't they? At op shops?

FI: I loved this dress. I wore it to Andrew Peacock's fortieth. Jim Killen told me I had marvellous legs.

LACHLAN: You do.

FI: Oh, you are such a sweet boy.

LACHLAN: I'm worried about Dad.

FI: Why, darling?

LACHLAN: I think he's losing the plot.

FI: Oh, don't worry about him. He was born to plot.

LACHLAN: People despise him, you know.

FI: He's always said—it's not about being liked. It's about being respected.

LACHLAN: They don't respect him. That's for sure. I walk into the ward-room and people stop talking suddenly. And I know why. I just say, 'Don't mind me. I hated him first.'

FI: Oh, darling.

LACHLAN: He's not really human. It's like he doesn't have a shame gland.

FI: Oh, Lockie, come on.

LACHLAN: No. It's true. Sometimes I think—what country am I from? Is this Algeria? I said to him the other night, I said, 'Dad you're turning us into some country like North Korea. Or Burma.' He just goes into his little sarcastic routine about trade relations and important intelligence networks between countries. It's all right for him. He takes a tough decision, he gets to be PM. But we're the ones doing his dirty work out there.

FI: [*holding up clothes*] Tsch. This is grubby. Oh, it's all grubby.

LACHLAN: You never ever challenge him.

FI: Oh, bloody hell. What is this? Don't tell me it's chewing gum? Oh, it is. It's chewing gum. Blast.

LACHLAN: Mum? Why don't you? Mum!

FI: Why don't I, what?

LACHLAN: Challenge him?

FI: Politics is a complex business, Lockie. Your father has to show that he'll do whatever it takes. That's what the electorate wants. They want a strong leader. They don't want uncertainty. They really don't. [*She pulls out Marty's rugby jumper from the box.*] Oh, my goodness. Oh. Oh.

LACHLAN: Marty's? [*Beat. He holds out his hand to take the jumper.*] Here.

   FI *shakes her head.*

FI: I know all Dad wants from you at this time is your loyalty.

   Beat.

LACHLAN: You make that sound so simple.

◆ ◆ ◆ ◆ ◆

SCENE NINE

JAMIE *paces around the office where* TOM *and* HAZEM *wait to see* EGGS.

JAMIE: This is highly irregular, Tom. If you'd like to come into my office—we'll talk in there—and I'll brief the Minister, later.

TOM: We'll wait. Thanks.

JAMIE: Mate, his diary is full.

TOM: Is that so?

JAMIE: You can't stay here. That's not an option.

TOM: You'll call security and have us removed?

JAMIE: Keep this up, Tom, and we'll be putting Mr Al Ayad on the first plane back to Iraq.

HAZEM: I think maybe we go.

TOM: You have that authority, do you Jamie?

JAMIE: Technically your friend—

TOM: My client.

JAMIE: Technically your client has breached his visa. People on Temporary Protection Visas can't just waltz in and out of Australia as they please.

HAZEM: I have not seen my family for four years. My wife she say, 'How many more year must we wait?' I say, 'You must be patient'. But is too late. She pay already money to the people smuggler.

> HAZEM *struggles to regain his composure.*

TOM: My client went to Indonesia to accompany his wife and his two daughters. It's a perilous journey.

JAMIE: An illegal journey.

TOM: As refugees seeking sanctuary, they had the protection of international law.

JAMIE: International lawyers do not make Australian law, Mr Benedict.

HAZEM: This no good this law. You say no family reunion. But the family must be together—is no right to say to man you cannot bring family. He go crazy.

JAMIE: Well, we certainly don't want to encourage crazy people. Especially not from the Middle East.

> *The door to* EGGS' *office opens and he strides towards* HAZEM *with his hand outstretched.*

EGGS: Mr Al Ayad. [*He uses two hands to demonstrate his deep compassion.*] Please accept my deepest sympathy for the loss of your family. You have suffered greatly. Please. Come through. Can I get you a cup of coffee?

HAZEM: No, thank you.

TOM: White, no sugar.

JAMIE: [*up close*] Get fucked.

TOM: Thanks, Jamie.

> JAMIE *walks off.*

EGGS: Did you just ask her to make you coffee?

TOM: I did.

EGGS: People have been shot for less.

HAZEM: [*Arabic*] La ili Allah ila Allah! [There is no God, but God!]

TOM: My client's a bit stunned at the high-handedness of your secretary.

EGGS: Since Iraq is leading the way in women's rights, I'm not surprised.

TOM: Thank you for agreeing to see my client… Minister.

EGGS: [*to* TOM] My pleasure… Mr Benedict. Do you want to wait outside? Unless you've learnt Arabic I think Mr Al Ayad and I can manage.

TOM: I'm his lawyer.

EGGS: Just as a matter of interest, are you planning to accompany the other twelve thousand people who want residency visas?

TOM: Probably. Until you start to honour your legal responsibilities.

EGGS: And what are they? In particular?

TOM: Protecting basic human rights would be a start.

EGGS: No, that's where you start. Top of my list is protecting Australia.

HAZEM: I want to live in this country. Here is good. This democracy.

TOM: My client would make a very fine Australian citizen.

HAZEM: I work hard. Good for eco-nomic. I no harm to people.

EGGS: Well, good for you, Mr Al Ayad.

TOM: Hazem, I think the Minister would like to hear what happened on the twenty-fifth of December (Christmas morning, in fact) when the *Kelepasan* capsized.

EGGS: All ears. Do go on, Mr Al Ayad.

HAZEM: All of us are in the water. People are screaming for help. And I see three ships. But they do not help.

EGGS: And how does that affect the government?

HAZEM: One was Australia Navy ship.

EGGS: How do you know that it was an Australian Navy ship?

HAZEM: It flies Australia flag.

EGGS: You saw that did you? At four a.m. You saw the flag?

HAZEM: Yes. Is dark. But big light—

EGGS: With respect, Mr Al Ayad, you'd been in the ocean all night. You were suffering terrible physical and psychological distress. It's much more likely that you imagined a ship.

HAZEM: No. I saw ship. Three ship.

EGGS: I can assure you that any Navy ship would have been in there like a shot. My own son is a naval officer and he's pulled hundreds of people like you out of the drink, Mr Al Ayad. There was no Navy ship.

HAZEM: You lie. There was Navy ship. And they let my family drown. They stand and watch—and my family is dead.

TOM: My client is very upset. Minister, all he wants is residency. He's an innocent man. He's been incarcerated in the Australian desert for three years. Then after two visits to the Review Tribunal and then the Federal Court he was found to be a legitimate refugee fleeing torture and death in his own country.

EGGS: And then he risks his visa by buzzing off to Indonesia.

TOM: This is a man who put his family above everything else. He makes not one, but two dangerous journeys on the sea to save his own life and that of his wife and their two little girls. But they die—just like his brother and all his extended family back in Iraq. What more does a man have to bear?

EGGS: What are you proposing?

TOM: Section 417 of the Migration Act, gives you the power to treat my client as a special case—and to grant him permanent residency.

EGGS: And why would I do that? So that Mr Al Ayad can go around slurring the honour of the Australian Navy?

TOM: No. To ensure that he doesn't. My client has been invited to tell his story on the *7.30 Report*. If there was a Navy ship—standing by…

EGGS: Tom…

TOM: My client, Minister, is very anxious not to jeopardise his application for permanent residency. If that were to be granted, then he has no wish to feed the media's appetite for scandal.

EGGS: I see. All right, Mr Al Ayad. You show that you are a man of peace and good will, and I give you my undertaking that I will look personally into your case. I'll put my best people on to it. If you are who you say you are, then you have nothing to fear.

He shows them out.

Thank you for coming by, Mr Benedict. Goodbye, Mr Al Ayad. All the best.

❖ ❖ ❖ ❖ ❖

SCENE TEN

Tom and Angela's house. ANGELA *is marking papers.* HARRY *is checking the cupboard.*

HARRY: No coffee. Bloody hell. How come there's no coffee?

ANGELA: I beg your pardon, Your Royal Highness. You'll have to make a supreme effort and walk to the corner shop.

HARRY: I've just walked all the way from the city.

ANGELA: What's the matter with you?

HARRY: Nothing.

ANGELA: Harry?

HARRY: I didn't get the tender.

ANGELA: Oh, sweetheart, I'm sorry.

HARRY: They gave it to that loser, Julian Wilks.

ANGELA: This is for the bar in the city? Oh, Harry.

HARRY: There wasn't a single person in that outfit who had a clue about contemporary design. You know how I told you they wanted a retro-futuristic look? They didn't. They chose this stained-glass mosaic on dark wood bullshit that's been shat into half the laneways in the CBD. It's so '98. But what would they know? No one's going to go there. I give it three months. Max.

ANGELA: That's really disappointing, Harry.

HARRY: Whatever. Just don't tell Dad. Please.

ANGELA: Why not?

HARRY: I can't handle the lecture.

ANGELA: He'll be understanding.

HARRY: No he won't. He thinks he knows everything about how the market place works. Understanding the client's needs. All that crap.

ANGELA: Well?

HARRY: He's a socialist, for God's sake.

ANGELA: He's going to have to know sooner or later.

HARRY: Why? He won't ask.

ANGELA: You haven't got a job.

HARRY: I don't want to be a salary man. Doing corporate shit. I want to do my own work. We've had this conversation. It's just that you and Dad don't think I'm good enough.

ANGELA: It's not that.

HARRY: Yeah. Whatever, Mum.

> HARRY *exits.* ANGELA *sighs and goes back to her work. She hears a thump outside and then sees a shadow moving across the wall. She is frozen. She goes to investigate and bumps into a very drunk* LACHLAN. ANGELA *screams.*

LACHLAN: Sorry. Sorry.

ANGELA: Jesus, Lachlan.

LACHLAN: Sorry.

ANGELA: You gave me the fright of my life.

LACHLAN: I didn't want to wake you up.

ANGELA: It's only nine-thirty.

LACHLAN: I've had a bit to drink.

ANGELA: You don't say. [*Beat.*] Is everything okay?

LACHLAN: No. I don't think so. Is Tom here?

ANGELA: I'll get him.

> ANGELA *exits and calls for* TOM. LACHLAN *is agitated—and alone in the room.* TOM *enters.*

TOM: Hey, Lock.

LACHLAN: I can't do this anymore, Tom.

TOM: What's that, Lock?

LACHLAN: I can't… lie anymore.

TOM: Okay. Fair enough. [*Beat.*] Want some coffee?

LACHLAN: No. I want to stop all the bullshit. There's too much. Isn't there? In the world?

TOM: Mm-hmm. Sure is. No argument there.

LACHLAN: No one tells the truth. Have you noticed this? Now. Aunty Ange. She does.

TOM: She sure does.

LACHLAN: No… I like that. About Annie Ange. Great arse too.

TOM: I'll say.

LACHLAN: I was thinking maybe I'd work in a bar.

TOM: Uh-huh. Makes a change from the Navy.

LACHLAN: Listen. I'm a Navy man. I *fit* in the Navy and I'm not sure I'm gonna *fit* anywhere else. But I can't be in the Navy. [*Beat.*] You can't just let people die. It's not even war.

TOM: What people?

LACHLAN: You think you know all about it. But you haven't got the faintest idea what's happening out there.

TOM: Tell me.

LACHLAN: I don't know what to do, Tom.

TOM: I can help.

LACHLAN: You didn't help Marty.

TOM: No I didn't. But what happened to Marty was an accident.

LACHLAN: It's screwed everyone round.

TOM: I know. Lockie. Who died?

LACHLAN: Why? So you can score points against my father?

TOM: Lockie, tell me. What's happening out there?

LACHLAN: Christmas morning, right? Gunnery Officer Peters wakes me up. He goes, 'A boat's gone down'. I said, 'Have we rescued them?' And he said, 'No. We've gone about. We're heading back to Ashmore Reef.'

TOM: The *Kelepasan*?

LACHLAN *nods.*

LACHLAN: And I go on deck and there were people in the sea. And we were turning away. None of us could believe it. I can't think what to do. Everyone's saying we've been ordered to back off. So I ring my father. And he says, 'This is totally inappropriate'. And I go, 'I'll tell you what's fucking inappropriate'.

TOM: And he hung up.

LACHLAN: He did. He hung up.

Beat.

TOM: You're sure about this?

LACHLAN: Yeah.

TOM: On Christmas morning?

LACHLAN: Yes.

TOM: I just can't… Would you say this publicly?

LACHLAN: About Dad?

TOM: About the whole thing.

LACHLAN: No. Jesus. Are you kidding?

TOM: Why not?

LACHLAN: I'll get court-martialled.

TOM: Have they threatened you?

LACHLAN: You can't talk about these kind of operations.

TOM: People died out there.

LACHLAN: I know. I fucking know, Tom.

TOM: Who's behind this? Is it Eggs?

Beat.

LACHLAN: He said it was nothing to do with him.

◆ ◆ ◆ ◆ ◆

SCENE ELEVEN

Eggs' office. EGGS *is running on a treadmill.*

EGGS: Bloody hell. Jamie. Is this… absolutely… necessary?

JAMIE: Yes. Come on, Eggs. You're not even sweating.

EGGS: No. Piss off.

JAMIE: The Prime Minister walks. You *run.*

EGGS: I'll be dead before the ballot.

     TOM *enters.*

TOM: You'll be dead sooner than that.

EGGS: Tom. It never occurs to you to make an appointment?

TOM: I know about the *Kelepasan.*

JAMIE: What is this? Groundhog Day?

TOM: The Navy was there.

EGGS: The closest Navy ship was a hundred nautical miles away.

TOM: It was not. There was a frigate right there and you know it.

JAMIE: The first thing we knew about the whole incident was when your
    mate showed up at the Jakarta docks. Rescued by a fishing boat.

TOM: Bullshit. A Navy boat was there. And you gave the order.

EGGS: *I* gave the order. What order was that?

TOM: 'Take no action.' That's what you said.

JAMIE: You're full of shit.

EGGS: What are you saying? I ordered a Navy boat not to attend a
    maritime emergency?

JAMIE: Why are we putting up with this?

EGGS: You are making this allegation—Jesus, Tom. Have you got any
    evidence? Or is this just some fantasy—?

TOM: I have my sources.

EGGS: He has his sources. / What a joke.

JAMIE: Who would they be?

EGGS: Come on, Tommy. Tell us who your 'sources' are.

TOM: It wasn't any Navy boat. It was the *Kalgoorlie.*

EGGS: Bloody hell.

JAMIE: In your dreams.

EGGS: The *Kalgoorlie* was five hours due south.

TOM: There are whistleblowers everywhere, Eggs. Even in the Navy.

Beat.

EGGS: Look. The Indonesian Coastwatch is responsible for that stretch of water.

TOM: That's bullshit and you know it.

EGGS: It wasn't up to us—

TOM: I make one phone call to the *Bulletin*—

EGGS: The boat went down in Indonesian waters.

TOM: It went down in international waters—well inside the Australian surveillance zone. And the *Kalgoorlie* turned about, because someone gave the order. And we both know who did that.

EGGS: What is it with you, Tom? You despise me so much that you honestly believe I would issue an order to let people drown in the ocean. I'm your brother. I can't tell you details about military intelligence. Obviously. Suffice to say—there is more going on than you can possibly understand. But, you know, none of that matters to me. The only thing that matters is that my own brother is making accusations about my *integrity*. That's really knocked me for six, Tom.

TOM: Then account for what happened on Christmas morning.

EGGS: No. I don't feel the slightest need to account for myself. Not to you. Not to anyone. But what you need to know is that I am now in a position where I cannot allow your Muslim mate / to stay here.

TOM: Oh, don't be a complete—

EGGS: The very fact that you would use him to destroy public confidence in me—that's / insupportable.

TOM: You wouldn't—you can't do this. This is—Eggs—

EGGS: There's too much at stake. You've really blown it this time, Tom. No. No. No. *No!* Believe me. He's on the first plane back to Iraq— that's the end of him.

TOM: This is morally corrupt what you're doing.

EGGS: I'll tell you what's corrupt. Your kind of moral blackmail that'll expose this country to full-scale ethnic violence. And that'll happen, Tom—you mark my words—if we don't have complete control of our immigration program.

TOM: This is just political hysteria and you know it. You spiteful bastard.

TOM *exits*

JAMIE: Who's he been talking to?

EGGS: Lockie. Obviously.

JAMIE: 'I have my sources.' Jesus wept.

EGGS: Tom's got to him. That's for sure. Bludgeoned it out of him.

JAMIE: Lockie's very impressionable.

EGGS: Leaking secret operational information. What's got into him?

JAMIE: I'll talk to the Chief of the Navy. Make sure none of the others get any bright ideas.

◆ ◆ ◆ ◆ ◆

SCENE TWELVE

Mid afternoon. TOM *knocks furiously at the door of Hazem's flat.*

TOM: Hazem! Quick! It's Tom! Open the door!

HAZEM: Tom—

TOM: Hazem. You've got to get out of here.

HAZEM: Why? What's happened?

TOM: They're going to deport you.

HAZEM: Deport? Not to Iraq?

TOM: We can fight this.

HAZEM: Oh, God. Please, God! Why you do this to me? This is too much. Why you no kill me before?

TOM: Hazem. Listen to me. You have to pack up all your stuff. They could come any time.

HAZEM: Your brother he say he give me visa. He promise.

TOM: He's changed his mind.

HAZEM: Why? I've done nothing.

TOM: I know. It's this whole cruel set-up. I went to see him this morning, to demand some answers.

HAZEM: You upset him. You make him angry.

TOM: That ship you saw in the night. It *was* a Navy ship.

HAZEM: I tell you.

TOM: I know you did. But I thought—

HAZEM: You thought what? I was lying?

TOM: Come on, Hazem. You must see. This is bigger than… just you. Your story could bring down the government. Don't you see? I had to know who was responsible for what / happened out there.

HAZEM: You use me for *politic*.

TOM: Hazem please. We haven't got time.

HAZEM: You use me to fight with him.

TOM: This is not about me and him.

HAZEM: My wife and my daughters died to come here.

TOM: I know. I know... And God spared you for a reason, remember. You have to tell your story.

HAZEM: I want to live. I just want to live.

TOM: Then we need the people to know.

HAZEM: No. I need to find a country where I can live. A home. A job. But I have to be citizen first.

TOM: All right. Let's not argue. We have to move quickly. We have a family beach house. / You'll be safe there.

HAZEM: You think I am fool? Is your family—your own brother—who wants me deport.

TOM: It'll be fine. The house is all locked up. Eggs is going to be in Canberra.

HAZEM: [*Arabic*] *Ya Allah. Wen inti? Wen inti, mut shoof?* [Oh God. Where are you? Where are you, don't you see what's happening?]

TOM: Look. I've hired a car for you. It's outside. Here's a map. And the key to the back door. I'll come down later tonight. We've got to buy some time so we can appeal to the court.

HAZEM *is not convinced.*

Mate, you've got no other choice.

◆ ◆ ◆ ◆ ◆

SCENE THIRTEEN

Friday night midnight. The remote seaside weekender of the Benedict family.

The cliff-top house is in darkness. A savage wind is blowing off the sea. Tyres on gravel. A sweep of headlights casts shadows in the main room.

Footsteps on the gravel. The external light switches on automatically, casting an eerie light in the room. There is the sound of the key in the door. It opens.

TOM *walks in.*

As he reaches for the light switch, a man leaps out of the shadows with a shriek. TOM *shouts out in terror until he sees it is* EGGS.

TOM: Jesus wept. You gave me the fright of my life. What are you doing here? I thought you were in Canberra this weekend.

EGGS: I thought you were... an intruder. I'm sorry. Christ. I'm sorry. [*Beat.*] What are you doing here?

TOM: I was meeting someone.

EGGS: Who?

TOM: Just someone.

EGGS: No. Nobody here. Just me.

TOM: I thought I saw a car pulling out of the driveway. Just then. So I drove like blazes to catch up, beeping the horn and everything, but he didn't stop.

    EGGS *checks the door nervously.*

We arranged to meet down here at nine. But I got caught up at this meeting and then I got a flat tyre on the freeway.

EGGS: There isn't anyone here.

TOM: Yeah. He must have got cold feet. What time did you get down?

EGGS: Not long. Just before you.

TOM: Maybe he came and left.

EGGS: I'm sorry, I should have checked with you first.

TOM: What's happened to the carpet?

EGGS: What carpet?

TOM: It's gone.

EGGS: I dunno. Maybe Fi. Maybe Fi's getting it replaced. You know what she's like.

TOM: You're shaking. Let's get a drink. I could have sworn that car came out of our driveway.

EGGS: Next door probably.

TOM: Must have been. Maybe I should ring him. [*Beat.*] Oh, look.

EGGS: What? What is it?

TOM: It's a piece of the vase.

EGGS: What vase?

TOM: The vase we gave Fi.

EGGS: So it is. The cleaner must have broken it.

TOM *gets out his mobile.*

TOM: I'm going to call him.

> *He presses the number. A phone rings. Both men freeze.* TOM *bends down and retrieves the ringing phone from under the sofa.*
>
> *Blackout.*

END OF ACT ONE

ACT TWO

SCENE ONE

The beach house at Warramee. TOM *holds the ringing phone. He turns it off.*

TOM: Where is he? What happened? Eggs? Where's Hazem?

EGGS: I don't know what you're talking about.

TOM: He was here.

EGGS: Fascinating how these people—who claim to be destitute—can afford a mobile phone.

TOM: Eggs?

EGGS: One of the great mysteries. Phones, videos, cars.

TOM: You've taken him.

EGGS: I've just arrived.

TOM: That car.

EGGS: What car?

TOM: That car coming out of the driveway.

EGGS: I didn't see any car.

TOM: You've taken him into detention.

EGGS: Oh, Tommy.

TOM: You've taken him. To Baxter or somewhere.

EGGS: Always quick with a conspiracy theory.

TOM: What have you done with him?

EGGS: In my experience when there's a choice between a conspiracy or a stuff-up—it's usually a stuff-up.

> JAMIE *enters. Both men jump.*

JAMIE: I came as / quickly… Jesus. Tom.

EGGS: Christ Almighty. Jamie?

TOM: Jesus Christ.

EGGS: She never knocks.

JAMIE: Are you okay?

EGGS: Tom was expecting a friend apparently.

JAMIE: Oh. Right.

EGGS: And he hasn't shown up.

JAMIE: Right.

EGGS: So he's feeling a bit agitato. As am I. So I suggest we have a drink. I didn't hear your car.

JAMIE: I parked down the bottom.

EGGS: I'm very glad you're here. You can reassure Tom that I had nothing to do with the disappearance of his Middle Eastern friend.

JAMIE: Which Middle Eastern friend is that?

TOM: What are you doing here?

JAMIE: I'm the Minister's senior adviser.

TOM: And that involves coming to our beach house at midnight?

JAMIE: It involves a high level of personal commitment.

TOM: Is that what you're calling it these days?

JAMIE: It is advisable that you leave this matter to me. That's best. Under the circumstances.

TOM: What circumstances?

JAMIE: Security. That's our first priority.

TOM: My first priority is to find out what's happened to Hazem Al Ayad.

JAMIE: Tom, how much do you actually know about this man?

TOM: What do you mean?

JAMIE: ASIO has a dossier on him, this thick. So we know quite a lot about him.

TOM: I'm sure you do.

JAMIE: None of it particularly savoury.

EGGS: He's been tracked by international intelligence agencies since 1998.

TOM: So has the Dalai Lama.

JAMIE: He's a major security threat.

TOM: Hazem is an ordinary man, wanting to live an ordinary life in a safe country.

JAMIE: People who want ordinary lives shouldn't get involved in extremist causes.

TOM: Come off it, Jamie. The guy's just a regular Muslim.

JAMIE: So you don't know about his Al Qaeda connections—

TOM: Oh, for Chrissake!

JAMIE: … His close friendship with a senior official in Saddam Hussein's Ministry of Information. [*Beat.*] See, I don't think you quite understand the gravity of the situation.

TOM: I understand the gravity of slandering innocent people.

EGGS: No one's ever tried to take your life. To kill you. / You know, with their hands around your neck.

JAMIE: Eggs!

TOM: Is that what's happened? Hazem tried to kill you?

JAMIE: This man is a trained killer.

EGGS: He came at me with a knife.

JAMIE: Eggs! Please!

TOM: And then what happened?

EGGS: The little bastard threatened me.

JAMIE: Eggs—

TOM: Eggs? What's happened to Hazem?

EGGS: He's dead.

TOM: Oh, my God. No.

EGGS: This is what happens—

JAMIE: Eggs!

EGGS: —when you lie in wait—

JAMIE: Eggs! Wait a minute

EGGS: —when you break in—

JAMIE: Stop it, Eggs!

EGGS: —and try and kill someone.

TOM: He had a key.

JAMIE: You need to let me take charge—

EGGS: That's what happens—

TOM: I gave him the key.

EGGS: You get what you deserve.

TOM: He was here to see me.

EGGS: He was here to slit my throat.

JAMIE: This must not go beyond—

EGGS: He was hiding behind—

JAMIE: —these four walls.

EGGS: He saw his chance to get his revenge—

JAMIE: Eggs!

EGGS: —and he tried to take it.

JAMIE: For God's sake! You don't talk to anyone without consulting me first. I trust I've made myself clear.

◆ ◆ ◆ ◆ ◆

SCENE TWO

At the home of Fi and Eggs.

FI: You've got three years to serve. They're not going to let you go.

LACHLAN: I talked to the 2IC. I said—You have to get me out of this. Fill out the forms. Otherwise it's dresses and the whole Klinger routine.

FI: Have you talked it over with Dad?

LACHLAN: Yeah, right.

FI: He has his share of doubts.

LACHLAN: He's never doubted anything in his life. Why do you always defend him when you know he sent Marty off the rails?

FI: Marty wasn't very strong.

LACHLAN: Neither am I.

FI: You are. You're a very strong person, Lockie. Don't say that. We're very proud of you.

LACHLAN: And when it comes to war, Lockie's the man you could sacrifice. Marty's death was a tragedy. Lockie's death would have you all cheering.

FI: That's not what we think.

LACHLAN: 'We think.' 'We think.' 'We think.' What's wrong with you? Can't you think for yourself?

FI: It's not what *I* think. And your father—

LACHLAN: My father thinks that I am a pathetic human being—

EGGS *whirls in.*

EGGS: Well, stop acting like one. For Chrissake. I've been speaking to the Chief of Defence. He told me what a very impressive young man you are. Information he gleaned from the Commander of your ship. So it'd be very tedious to have to tell them that you're a weak little shit.

FI: Eggs, don't do this.

LACHLAN: I have tried over and over to talk to you about what it's like out there—

EGGS: I don't care. And I want you to hear that loud and clear. It is no fun in Canberra either. / But you and I Lockie—we're made of the same stuff.

FI: Eggs—

LACHLAN: No we're not.

EGGS: Oh, yes / we are.

FI: Eggs, hear him out—

EGGS: We're fighters, you and me. Do you understand what I'm saying, Lachlan? We hold on / and we fight.

LACHLAN: But what you and I are doing is wrong.

EGGS: No. No. What you and I are doing requires fierce / strength of mind—

FI: Eggs, why are you doing / this? Why do you have to—?

EGGS: Fiona, do you mind—*do you mind*?! I'm talking / to my son.

LACHLAN: People died out there, Dad.

EGGS: People always die, Lachlan. People live and then they die. And the terrible failing about people like my brother is that they can't face it.

LACHLAN: I can't either.

EGGS: Oh, yes you can. Because inside here [*thumping him on the chest*] there's fire. We burn, you and me. We boil inside until our guts are blistered. But we never ever give up. Because we know we're the ones who have to take action. We're the ones who have to make decisions that affect a great many people's lives. And that means sometimes we have to make a decision that affects their deaths. Ever killed a man, Lock?

LACHLAN: No.

EGGS: But you wonder about it, don't you? Every man does. I have a gun. The enemy soldier has a gun. Can I pull the trigger? Some men can't, you know. They just can't do it. And they're the pricks who end up dead. [*He pulls out the knife.*] Do you recognise this?

LACHLAN: My fishing knife.

EGGS: Oh yeah, look. 'LB'. You burnt your initials in the handle. It's surprisingly easy, Lockie, when you stick the knife in. It's like the whole universe is resisting. Like when a plane takes off. Every rivet is straining and shuddering and all of nature is fighting against this massive thing straining to leave the earth. You think you'll never do it and then all of a sudden you're flying: the blade cuts through to the soft warm life inside. And the stupid prick is looking at you in disbelief. His eyes pop out like prawns. And you can feel the life flowing out of him and into you. My God, you've never felt so gloriously alive. Self-defence, Lachlan. One on one. Civilisation versus anarchy. Him or me.

He hands him the knife.

There you go, Mr Principal Warfare Officer. I've blooded it for you.

He leaves. Silence.

◆ ◆ ◆ ◆ ◆

SCENE THREE

Angela and Tom's house.

ANGELA: What's wrong?
TOM: Eggs killed someone.
ANGELA: What?
TOM: Eggs has killed Hazem Al Ayad.
ANGELA: In a car accident?
TOM: No.
ANGELA: What then?
TOM: With a knife.
ANGELA: Jesus.
TOM: There was a struggle.
ANGELA: Omigod.
TOM: It was self-defence.
ANGELA: Hazem.
TOM: He's dead.
ANGELA: Not Hazem. Poor little Hazem.
TOM: It was an accident. He didn't mean to.
ANGELA: I hate him. I hate your brother.
TOM: Ange. For Chrissake.
ANGELA: He killed a man.
TOM: Hazem came at Eggs with a knife.
ANGELA: He killed an asylum seeker. He stabbed / a man to death.
TOM: They're saying he was a trained killer. Al Qaeda.
ANGELA: That'd be right. / Bloody arseholes—honestly…
TOM: Associating with a terrorist. Giving him financial support. I'll be lucky not to go to jail.

ANGELA: What are you saying?

TOM: I could be locked up and interrogated by goons for a week—just because ASIO says that Hazem was a terrorist.

ANGELA: Oh, come on. As if they are going to arrest Tom Benedict, CEO of the Lawson Foundation.

TOM: Angela, if they have 'reasonable grounds' to think you have information that they want—they can work you over for a week.

ANGELA: Tom! You are the Minister's brother.

TOM: No. I'm the lawyer of the man who tried to assassinate him.

ANGELA: [*Greek*] *Scase re! Ti scatta milas!* [Shut up, you! What shit you are talking!]

TOM: My brother has just killed a man. Do you understand what I'm saying? My friend Hazem is dead on a slab in some government morgue. And my brother did this. My brother. My own brother. Do you understand that this is as bad as if I'd killed him myself?

◆ ◆ ◆ ◆ ◆

SCENE FOUR

Eggs' office. It is Sunday. EGGS *and* JAMIE *are wearing weekend clothes.*

JAMIE: We could go public on this, Eggs.

EGGS: Yeah, sure. Great idea.

JAMIE: Hear me out.

EGGS: I am being advised by a frigging nuff-nuff.

JAMIE: Just listen.

EGGS: Why? I've been listening all morning.

JAMIE: It goes like this: This Arab terrorist—

EGGS: I killed a man. Hasn't that penetrated your thick skull? A man is dead and you want me to go to the Australian people and confess that I did this. With a knife. Just the man they'd want for Prime Minister.

JAMIE: An Arab terrorist with links to Al Qaeda—used your brother to get to you. You arrived at your beach house on Friday evening and this maniac jumped you.

EGGS: He did.

JAMIE: So we are no longer safe. In our own homes. But you have faced the enemy and triumphed.

EGGS: Sometimes I think you're not the full quid.

The intercom buzzes.

ERIC: [*voice-over on the intercom*] Minister. I've got Bob Fuller on the phone.

EGGS: Tell him to piss off.

JAMIE: Put him through. [*To* EGGS] You need his vote.

EGGS: What's he after?

JAMIE: Foreign Affairs.

EGGS: [*spluttering*] Un-fucking-believable. He'll get the High Commission in Wellington. If he's lucky.

JAMIE: If you get Bob Fuller, you'll nail the other four in Tasmania.

EGGS: I've promised Knuckles Carson Deputy Speaker.

JAMIE: So who's Speaker?

EGGS: Not Bob Fuller. That's for sure. [*Into the phone*] Bob. How are you, ol' son? Now before you say a thing, I want you to know that I did have you in mind for Foreign Affairs. But, frankly, I'll need someone of your experience on the ground in Tassie. I'll need your knowledge and grass roots expertise. Uh-huh. No problem. Oh, by the way, Andrew Romsey's got a share in a horse you might be interested in. It's had a couple of good wins in the bush. Yep. Board membership? Gee, that's tricky. I'll have a word to Ari Grossman at Bilson. No harm topping up your super, eh Bob? Good on you, mate. [*He hangs up.*] Gotcha! Four more and I've got the numbers. Now how are we gonna to kill this other crap?

JAMIE: How far do you think Tom's prepared to take this?

Beat.

EGGS: This is a man who once rode a bicycle across the Nullarbor Plain.

JAMIE: Tom?

EGGS: Ten years ago. He was raising awareness for some Aboriginal nonsense.

Beat.

JAMIE: Then we're going to have to do things that you won't like.

EGGS: Like what?

JAMIE: Leave it to me.

EGGS: Meaning?

JAMIE: I'll handle it.

◆ ◆ ◆ ◆ ◆

SCENE FIVE

Angela and Tom's. HARRY *enters.*

HARRY: I can't handle it.

TOM: What?

HARRY: I had blond tips done on the weekend and they've gone green. Haven't they? I look like a freak.

ANGELA: You should've gone back to the hairdresser.

HARRY: I did. And this stupid girl goes, 'There's nothing I can do about it'. Such a bitch. She said, 'It's obviously the chlorine in the pool'. / Which is such crap—

The doorbell rings.

ANGELA: Who could that be?

  ANGELA *exits.*

TOM: Harry—

HARRY: —I haven't even been to the pool. Just the gym.

TOM: Harry! I'm in the middle of something here.

HARRY: Full on. Should I make an appointment?

TOM: I know it's a national scandal about your hair—

  He is interrupted by ANGELA*'s return with* JAMIE.

Jamie!

JAMIE: Well. The whole fam—damly.

  Beat.

TOM: You know my son Harry?

JAMIE: Green hair?

HARRY: Yeah.

JAMIE: [*to* TOM] Can we talk in private?

TOM: We can talk here.

  Beat.

JAMIE: I don't think so.

ANGELA: We know what happened.

JAMIE: Who else does?

ANGELA: Nobody. Yet.

JAMIE: What you need to understand—all of you—is that you are in an extremely dangerous situation. The attack on your brother on Friday night was an act of terrorism.

HARRY: Hazem was a terrorist?

JAMIE: He was a Muslim fundamentalist—

ANGELA: He was a moderate!

JAMIE: —who attacked a member of the government—with a knife.

HARRY: Full on. Is she for real?

ANGELA: It's their word against ours. [*To* JAMIE] But you never have to come up with any evidence—do you, Jamie?—because that's all hush-hush. National security.

JAMIE: Angela, I'm doing you a favour. Okay? You're in this up to your neck and they'll take you into custody if they consider it necessary.

HARRY: They can't do that.

JAMIE: Watch them.

TOM: Jamie, there were lots of people who knew that Hazem was going down to Warramee.

JAMIE: Like who?

TOM: The Iraqi community. People at the Lawson Foundation.

ANGELA: A man doesn't just disappear.

TOM: Perhaps he does in Jamie's world. Who do you call when you want to dispose of a body? ASIO? The Federal Police?

ANGELA: Do government ministers have their own special pin number?

HARRY: This is surreal.

JAMIE: No. This is real, Shrek. Very, very real.

> HARRY *bristles.*

I think you should know, Tom, that the funding arrangements for the Lawson Foundation are very tenuous. Perhaps you don't fully appreciate that there are conditions attached to your subsidy.

ANGELA: Meaning what?

JAMIE: Meaning, we give you money to provide welfare services. We do not give you money to slag off the government.

TOM: We need to do more than hand out soup and blankets, Jamie. It's my job to represent my clients' interests to government.

JAMIE: You just don't get it, do you? Let me lay it on the line. This government is not in the business of funding you to be a professional bleeding heart. First it was the Stolen Generation, then it was global warming and now it's the refugees. Where do you get off?

HARRY: I think that tells you he is motivated by something other than self-interest.

JAMIE: It tells me he's made a career out of grandstanding on trendy lefty issues.

HARRY: What are you on about?

TOM: Apparently, none of us believe in anything. We've just created jobs for ourselves by pretending that some things matter.

JAMIE: The point is, we've had it up to here, mate. So if you don't belt up, I'm telling you—your recurrent funding?—down the toilet.

TOM: You'd cut federal funding to the Lawson Foundation?

JAMIE: You side with terrorists, my friend, and we'll shut you down. Make it easy on yourselves. The man is dead.

ANGELA: Eggs desperately wants to be PM.

JAMIE: Which makes him a very dangerous man, Angela. Be smart— take Tom to Brussels.

JAMIE *leaves.*

TOM: All of a sudden the world is run by ghastly women with impeccable grooming.

ANGELA: Where did they all come from?

TOM: Sydney, I expect.

HARRY: What happens if they cut your funding?

ANGELA: [*to* HARRY] He'll have to go the way of Greenpeace. Or Amnesty. They're independent of government for precisely this reason.

TOM: Except that they don't have three hundred thousand families who are dependent on them for basic services.

HARRY: What are you going to do?

TOM: I am going to do what I always do when some nasty little bully threatens me.

HARRY: What?

TOM: Fight back.

◆ ◆ ◆ ◆ ◆

SCENE SIX

Eggs' office. TOM *makes his way defiantly towards the Minister's office, despite protestations from the Minister's media advisor,* ERIC.

ERIC: [*offstage*] Excuse me, Mr Benedict. Excuse me. The Minister's in a meeting.

    TOM *barges in to find* EGGS *and* JAMIE *having sex on his desk.*

EGGS: Christ Almighty.

JAMIE: Bloody hell.

    They scramble to get their clothes back on, but TOM *doesn't move.*

EGGS: Do you mind?

TOM: I need to talk to you.

EGGS: Well, I really don't need to talk to you. And not now.

TOM: I'll wait.

EGGS: See what I mean?

JAMIE: Un-fucking-believable.

TOM: I'm not going to talk in front of her.

EGGS: I'm not going to talk, full stop. Now, piss off.

TOM: She is utterly corrupt—

JAMIE: Fuck off.

TOM: Utterly without conscience—

JAMIE: Get over it, Tom—

EGGS: Come off it, Tom.

TOM: —and apparently in complete control. But no amount of lying and bullying from her is gonna keep you safe. Because people will find out, sooner or later.

JAMIE: Nobody is going to find out. And even if they did—they don't care. Because they don't like these Muslims. And they don't want them here.

TOM: Not liking them is a far cry from killing them.

JAMIE: Two hundred and fifty people drowned in that boat. Has there been wailing in the streets? I don't think so.

EGGS: He's not concerned with public opinion.

JAMIE: Obviously.

TOM: You have to say that Hazem died in our house.

JAMIE: He'll say nothing of the sort.

TOM: If you don't come clean, it'll look as if you're covering up.

JAMIE: He is covering up.

TOM: There has to be a coronial enquiry.

JAMIE: No there doesn't.

TOM: Don't you ever shut up?

EGGS: Jamie, if you don't mind—

TOM: No one's interested. Eggs. Please.

EGGS: I need to talk to Tom.

JAMIE: This is not a good idea.

EGGS: Just five minutes.

TOM: Run along now, Jamie.

JAMIE: We need to make a full statement about the cash-for-visas business.

EGGS: Jamie.

JAMIE: The media is wanting a response. You don't have time to help your brother with his panic attacks.

EGGS: Two minutes.

> JAMIE *exits, slamming the door.*

TOM: I hate that woman.

EGGS: Oh, Jesus Christ, Tom. Just stop for a minute.

TOM: What happened on Christmas morning?

EGGS: We were at Warramee.

TOM: You ordered the *Kalgoorlie* turn about.

EGGS: We're not in the business of search and rescue.

TOM: So you have power over life and death.

EGGS: I'm the Minister for Home Security. It's my job to keep Australia safe.

TOM: And last Friday night you killed a man. [*He stares at his brother, implacable.*] Completely confident that there will be no enquiry into either incident.

EGGS: It's not in the national interest.

TOM: Listen to yourself. You're sounding like Stalin.

EGGS: Any jury in the world would say it was self-defence.

TOM: This is a democracy, you arsehole.

EGGS: Legally I am in the clear.

TOM: You killed my friend.

EGGS *grabs him.*

EGGS: And next Monday I fly to Canberra and I go into a room and sixty-five people cast their vote and fifteen minutes later I walk out into the Canberra sunshine—the Prime Minister of this country.

TOM: Our mother would weep if she knew. I promised her. We stood in the kitchen when Dad told us how sick she was and Mum said, 'Promise me that you two will always be there for each other. No matter what.' Remember? I can't do that anymore. And she wouldn't want me to, either.

EGGS: Yes, she would. No matter what.

❖ ❖ ❖ ❖ ❖

SCENE SEVEN

In the darkness, a figure is pacing. It is an eerie night. A curtain blows out an open window. Wind is prowling with tomcats.

FI *appears in an open door. We see that the figure is* EGGS.

EGGS: You know what they say about callous bastards? They sleep like babies. I killed a man, Fi. My son is frightened of me, my brother feels nothing but contempt, and my wife despises me. I've never felt so alone in my life.

FI: Perhaps you should go and see your mistress, then.

EGGS: Who might that be?

FI *laughs sourly.*

She has a husband.

FI: How inconvenient.

EGGS: There is nothing going on between Jamie and me. But what the hell. Why take my word for it? Let's give her a ring and she can tell you, herself. [*He grabs his mobile phone and says (voice recognition):*] 'Jamie'.

FI: It is half past four.

EGGS: Jamie works for me, Fiona. And if her job is to reassure my wife at half past four in the morning… [*Into the mobile*] Jamie. Fiona wants a quiet word.

He holds out the mobile. FI *does not move.*

[*Into the mobile*] Sorry. She's gone all shy. Look, she needs to know that you and I have never had intimate sexual relations. So perhaps you could just let her know that you have never put your mouth anywhere near my anatomy. [*To* FI] Have I got this right, Fiona? [*Into the mobile*] Despite the fact she's frigid as a corpse, she wants to make sure that I'm not having the time of my life screwing you senseless. Hold on will you, Jamie, I'll just put the old girl on.

FI *walks out. He calls after her:*

Not feeling friendly anymore, Fiona? Feeble? [*Into the mobile*] Sorry, Jamie—it seems the crisis has passed. Sweet dreams. [*He hangs up. Beat. Calling out*] What else can I do, to help you with your tenuous grip on reality?

FI *comes back.*

FI: I want to be free of you.

EGGS: Only four more days.

FI: And then?

EGGS: Keep the faith. I will be a great Prime Minister.

FI: You ordered Lockie's Commander to abandon those people, didn't you?

EGGS: This is not your concern.

FI: I heard you—we all did—on Christmas Day.

EGGS: I will not be interrogated by my own wife.

FI: Then perhaps you shouldn't behave like a vicious thug.

EGGS: Do you know what makes a great PM, Fiona?

FI: I couldn't care less.

EGGS: He understands that not everything that troubles people's consciences is inherently wrong. In fact doing what is right can incur terrible costs. But he has to tough it out. And by the time he dies, he's so thoroughly overcome the dangers that faced him, that it is difficult to recall the magnitude of those dangers, or even the magnitude of his achievements. But he has cast the future security and prosperity of his nation. You've really only got one option Fiona: stand up straight—and start behaving like my wife.

◆ ◆ ◆ ◆ ◆

SCENE EIGHT

TOM *is addressing the National Press Club.*

TOM: Ladies and gentlemen of the National Press Club. I have a vivid memory from my kindergarten days in Beaumaris. My brother is standing triumphantly on the top of the slide and he's pushing away any other kids who want to climb up the ladder.

Of course I am in the sandpit—playing collaboratively with the other children.

Laughter.

And now, as everyone knows, James Eggs Benedict is once again standing on the top of the slide—which is why you're all wondering if brother Tom is going to pull his head in.

Well, members of the National Press Club, I hope your pencils are sharp.

Four months ago, two hundred and fifty men, women and children were killed when the *Kelepasan* sank in waters between Indonesia and Australia. These families were risking their lives to escape the peril of their homelands. They wanted, more than anything else, to do as our forebears did—to find new lives in Australia.

I want to tell you about one of these aspiring Australians—an Iraqi named Hazem Al Ayad. He was on the *Kelepasan* the night it sank. Hazem was in the ocean, clinging to life, when he saw the Australian naval frigate *Kalgoorlie* a short distance across the water. The *Kalgoorlie* was there.

And it turned away. Just as we have all turned away. While, in our name, this government has committed acts of senseless cruelty on people who in all humanity deserve our compassion.

And now my friend Hazem—this witness to that act—is also dead.

No one has been held to account for all these deaths—not by the press, not by the law, not by the court of public opinion. The government says there was no ship. They deny that they were in any way responsible for this tragedy. So I say, let them tell us what actually happened. Let us have the truth.

So today, ladies and gentlemen, I do speak out—in support of my dead brother, Hazem Al Ayad—a man who taught me the words of Martin Luther King: 'Our lives begin to end the day we become silent about things that matter.'

◆ ◆ ◆ ◆ ◆

SCENE NINE

JAMIE *and* EGGS *watch* TOM *on TV.*

TOM: [*voice-over from the television*] In the name of law, humanity and our national honour, I am calling for an independent judicial inquiry into the deaths of all these aspiring Australians. Thank you.

>   *Applause.* JAMIE *turns it off.*

EGGS: Well, isn't that great. Thank heavens for my little brother. Now every journalist in the country will be onto this. Within twelve hours I'll be sacked and charged with the death of that little Iraqi bastard.

JAMIE: For God's sake, Eggs. Keep your head.

EGGS: Stupid me to panic when my whole political career has just come crashing down around my fucking head.

JAMIE: Everything is under control.

EGGS: Everything is in fucking chaos.

JAMIE: Mate, he didn't name you. He's a wimp. He doesn't have the bottle.

>   *The intercom buzzes.*

ERIC: [*voice-over on the intercom*] Minister, ABC radio on the line. John Ryan.

EGGS: [*to the intercom*] Tell him to go pull himself.

JAMIE: [*to the intercom*] Put him on, Eric. [*To* EGGS] Do the Bali speech.

EGGS: [*picking up the phone*] Good morning, John… You're very welcome… John, let me explain it this way…

>   *Eggs' mobile rings.* JAMIE *fishes in his pockets and takes it out.*

… in the face of tragedy it is a natural human impulse to want to blame. But the truth is, this was an accident. And those people made a choice.

JAMIE: [*answering the mobile*] Minister's phone.

EGGS: [*on the phone*] No. All I'm saying is that it is totally unacceptable, John. These brave young men and women are defending Australia's borders.

JAMIE: [*into the mobile*] He's just doing radio, Prime Minister. Yes. Yes.

EGGS: [*on the phone*] And let me ask you this, John—where were the bleeding hearts when terrorists blew up the Sari Club in Bali in 2002? Eighty-eight young Australians died. But did we hear the professional protesting class jump up and down about that? I don't think so.

JAMIE: [*into the mobile*] He'll ring you straight back.

JAMIE *hangs up.*

EGGS: [*on the phone*] Always a pleasure, John. [*He hangs up.*] Socialist prick.

JAMIE: That was the PM.

The intercom buzzes.

EGGS: Jesus Christ!

JAMIE: Stupid old cunt.

Caroline Brazier as Jamie and Garry McDonald as Eggs in the 2005 STC / MTC production. (Photo: Jeff Busby)

EGGS: Did you learn to speak like that at St Catherine's?

The intercom buzzes again.

JAMIE: [*into the intercom*] Hold all calls, Eric.

Eggs' mobile rings.

EGGS: [*into the moblie*] What?! Neil! Good morning. No. Not at all. Never too busy to talk to the good people who listen to Neil MacMillan!

❖ ❖ ❖ ❖ ❖

SCENE TEN

Angela and Tom's house. ANGELA *is listening to* EGGS *on radio talking to Neil Mitchell.*

EGGS: [*voice-over on radio*] Neil. Political debate is a very healthy thing. We were raised on it. Our father made us debate at the table every night after dinner so I have had fifty years of debating my brother. And he has spent an equal amount of time losing the argument with me. So nothing has changed.

Laughter.

ANGELA: [*to the radio*] Very funny, *malaka*.

She switches it off. TOM *enters in a rage.*

TOM: What is it with the media in this country?

ANGELA: Not good?

TOM: Not good? It's a scandal. Eggs has issued a press release saying that Hazem has been sighted in an Al Qaeda training camp in Northern Afghanistan.

ANGELA: What about your Press Club speech?

TOM: It's like it never happened. Oh—except for this: 'I don't believe that Tom Benedict is an evil man. I prefer to think he is merely naïve. As Neville Chamberlain was naïve. Mr Benedict should go back to his soup kitchen and leave the job of running the country to his brother.'

ANGELA: What do you expect? It's Andrew Blott.

TOM: They've got the press sewn up. No one's interested anymore. It's outrageous. There should be a full public enquiry.

ANGELA: At least the ABC broadcast your speech.

TOM: Yeah, well that's got to stop. I don't know where else to turn, Ange. [*Beat.*] It's like the entire nation is complicit in letting him get away with it.

ANGELA: Hazem was not the only eyewitness to what happened out there.

◆ ◆ ◆ ◆ ◆

SCENE ELEVEN

At Tom and Angela's house.

LACHLAN: You should have seen him, Tom. I think he's gone mad. He was pacing around like a loony. 'It was civilisation versus anarchy.'

TOM: Was he pissed?

LACHLAN: No. Stone cold sober.

TOM: Jesus.

LACHLAN: What do we do, Tom? We can't say anything.

TOM: Why not?

LACHLAN: Because. You know why. He's my old man. I'm not going to dob him in.

TOM: I know that, Lock. He's my brother, don't forget. But how many more atrocities will there have to be, before someone speaks out?

LACHLAN: You're speaking out.

TOM: Someone who saw it with their own eyes.

LACHLAN: You're asking me to betray my own father.

TOM: I'm asking you to tell the truth.

LACHLAN: You have no idea how deep this goes.

TOM: I think I do.

LACHLAN: You can't ask me to do this.

TOM: I'm appealing to you as a man of honour.

LACHLAN: He was honouring what the Australian people want.

TOM: Not all the people.

LACHLAN: For Chrissake. A bus goes over a cliff in India—sixty people are killed—no one here chokes on their Weeties. Kids die by the thousands in Africa every day.

TOM: This is totally different. These people died because your father wants to be Prime Minister.

LACHLAN: Don't lecture me. There was an ocean of corpses out there. I see it every damn night.

TOM: So why did it happen? Why?

LACHLAN: Because—we have to make a stand.

TOM: It happened because your father is playing the politics of prejudice and fear.

LACHLAN: Just stop. All right? Stop. Don't put this on me. There were hundreds of witnesses on the *Kalgoorlie*. Just please leave me out of this.

TOM: But you are the man with the most reason to speak the truth.

LACHLAN: Mate, I have every reason to shut the fuck up.

TOM: You'll have all my support.

LACHLAN: I'm not going to be a traitor.

TOM: Your father has committed a crime against humanity.

LACHLAN: And I am his son.

TOM: Lockie, he has blood on his hands.

LACHLAN: Mate, this is all about blood.

◆ ◆ ◆ ◆ ◆

SCENE TWELVE

Tom and Angela's house. ANGELA *enters with* FI *into the kitchen.*

FI: I bought these documents for Tom. He asked me to sign them.

ANGELA: This is for the Lawson housing project?

FI: He's not here by any chance?

ANGELA: No.

FI: I thought you might like these.

> *She hands her a cake tin.*

ANGELA: *Kourabiethes.*

FI: I got the recipe from the *Women's Weekly.*

> *Beat.*

ANGELA: Let's have one with coffee.

FI: You're not too busy? I was just on my way to Collins Street. I thought I'd better buy myself a new frock. In case I have to be the Prime Minister's wife.

ANGELA: You sound like your heart's not in it.

FI: I find myself dreaming of jumping on a plane to Paris to see my sister, Johanna. Silly, isn't it?

ANGELA: Why don't you?

FI: I haven't been able to talk to Jo about what happened at the beach house… She'd find it completely grotesque.

ANGELA: Which it is.

FI: Her husband Jean-Pierre is terribly sweet. He repairs violins. I want so much to put some clothes in a bag and just disappear. You know. Just vanish. I see myself sitting in the window of a train, whizzing through France. Quite free of all of this hateful business. But the Prime Minister's wife can't just disappear, can she? They'd send out the dogs. Johanna used to love Eggs. Everybody did. But now she looks at me—just like you're looking at me—with a mixture of pity and bewilderment.

ANGELA: I don't mean to.

FI: It's okay. You're lucky. You don't know what it's like having to get into bed with a man you…

ANGELA: It hasn't always been plain sailing, you know. With Tom. All that Geraldine Blake business. Don't you remember?

FI: Not really.

ANGELA: He moved in with her. For six months. When Harry was at kindergarten. He had a lot of women back then, Tom. He even had a fling with that bitch, Jamie. Works for Eggs.

FI: No!

ANGELA: At some Labor Conference. He's not above sleeping with the enemy.

FI: Hard to imagine what men see in her.

ANGELA: Tom reckons she's a dud bash.

FI: She'll be running the country if things go badly on Monday.

ANGELA: You'll go to Canberra, I suppose. To smile and wave. And make the victory sign to the TV cameras.

FI: Of course. You know me. Loyal to the end. [*Beat.*] If my parents were alive they'd be thinking, 'Hasn't Fiona done well for herself. She's going to be the Prime Minister's wife'… [*She starts to cry.*] Oh, I'm sorry. I'm so sorry. [*She attempts to collect herself.*] I get depressed.

ANGELA: Yes.

FI: Last night I was driving my car along Beach Road and I had to summon every ounce of my strength not to turn the wheel and drive into the oncoming traffic.

ANGELA: Oh, Fi.

FI: I'm trapped with this man and if I don't toe the line, what's stopping him from getting rid of me?

ANGELA: Fi. You mustn't go back there. Come and stay with us.

FI: I can't.

ANGELA: Yes you can.

FI: What about Lockie?

ANGELA: Lockie can look after himself.

FI: I don't think so. I can't do this.

ANGELA: What time will Eggs get home?

FI: Eight o'clock. Nine.

ANGELA: Go home. Pack a bag and Tom will come and get you at seven.

◆ ◆ ◆ ◆ ◆

SCENE THIRTEEN

Tom and Angela's house. HARRY *enters.*

HARRY: I've been set up.

TOM: What?

HARRY: I've been set up!

TOM: What happened?

HARRY: I was driving out the South Eastern. Just past Monash, when this car pulled out from the on-ramp—

ANGELA: What sort of car?

HARRY: I thought they were police. It was a black Commodore. But there was no siren or anything. They just flashed their lights and indicated to pull over. These two guys get out. Real thugs. And one of them leans in the window and asks for my licence. The other one goes, 'Keys'. So I give him the keys and he goes round to the boot and comes back with this box—full of Ecstasy tablets—

ANGELA: Oh, Harry.

HARRY: I swear to God—that was the first time I'd seen them.

TOM: Go on.

HARRY: You believe me, don't you?

TOM: Keep going.

HARRY: Dad, I don't do drugs anymore. You know that.

TOM: Harry. I need to hear what happened.

HARRY: No, fuck it. You don't believe me. I have not touched anything for two years. / Someone is setting me up.

ANGELA: Harry, calm down. Just tell us what happened.

HARRY: The fat one goes, 'No relation to Eggs Benedict, I trust'. I didn't know what to say. I didn't want to involve Eggs in anything, so I just go, 'What's it to you?' and the other one, opens the door, and starts to pull me out of the car, but the belt was still on. Check this out.

He shows a bruise on his collar bone.

ANGELA: Jesus.

HARRY: Then the bald one hauls me up against the car and he says, 'You're in big trouble, smart arse. This is going to land you fifteen years.' Then the other one shouts at me, 'I'm going to ask you again. Are you any relation to the Member of Parliament?' The bald one's freaking me out so I tell them, 'Yes. He's my uncle'.

TOM: Then what happened?

HARRY: They let go. Just like that. And then the fat one goes, 'We raid your house. We find shit in your bedroom, you're dead. Get my drift?' And then they get in their car and piss off.

ANGELA: Oh, Harry.

Silence.

TOM: I'm going to ask you just once. Are you back on drugs?

Silence.

Are you dealing?

HARRY: I told you. I don't do drugs.

TOM: I want to believe you, Harry.

HARRY: Do you think if I was dealing that I'd be telling you all this?

ANGELA: This is Eggs.

TOM: Ssh.

ANGELA: Eggs is putting the frighteners on us.

TOM: Just shut up for once.

ANGELA: No, you shut up. / Eggs has set this up.

TOM: Angela, please. You didn't get the tender and Mum says you've taken a personal loan to pay off your Mastercard.

HARRY: So? I'm not selling drugs to deal with my debts—if that's what you're getting at.

TOM: Now's not the time to lie, Harry.

HARRY: You have never trusted me, have you?

TOM: Trust has to be earned.

ANGELA: Tom. What are you saying? Your son is being framed.

TOM: My son is in trouble.

ANGELA: And you turn against him?

TOM: I am trying to think this through.

ANGELA: You could start by trusting what he says.

TOM: Don't do this, Ange. It's not helping.

> HARRY *makes to exit.*

Where are you going?

HARRY: Out.

> HARRY *leaves. The door slams.*

ANGELA: Nice work.

TOM: He's let us down before.

ANGELA: And he's learnt his lesson. This is Eggs' doing.

TOM: But is it? How can we be sure?

ANGELA: Harry is your son. You stand by him.

◆ ◆ ◆ ◆ ◆

SCENE FOURTEEN

Eggs' office.

EGGS: You never met Marty, did you?

JAMIE: No.

EGGS: He was one out of the bag. He had everything going for him, you know. He was pretty wild at times. But there was a real style about that kid. He had pluck. He wasn't your plodder—like Lockie. Sometimes when I'm with Tom's kid—

JAMIE: Harry?

EGGS: I think—why Marty? My son is dead and that little squirt is still alive.

JAMIE: Life's a bitch.

EGGS: He's got this pathetic arrogance about him. Gives me the shits.

JAMIE: I know. Ghastly.

EGGS: It's because he's such a weak little pissant.

JAMIE: He's not a Benedict.

EGGS: No.

The intercom buzzes.

ERIC: [*voice-over on the intercom*] Minister, your son's here.

EGGS: Shit! [*To the intercom*] Okay. Show him in.

JAMIE: What now?

LACHLAN *enters.*

EGGS: Hi, Lockie. How's it going?

LACHLAN: Can I speak to you?

EGGS: I'm in a meeting.

LACHLAN: It'll only take a minute.

EGGS: Fire away.

JAMIE: Don't mind me.

EGGS: She knows everything there is to know about me.

LACHLAN: Harry's just got busted.

EGGS: Really?

LACHLAN: Do you know anything about this?

EGGS: No.

LACHLAN: Ange reckons you planted drugs in the boot of his car.

EGGS: Angela told you this, did she? I think we both know, Lachlan, that she is a very stupid woman. So I would take that with a grain of salt.

LACHLAN: Harry is my cousin.

EGGS: So?

LACHLAN: Don't do this, Dad.

JAMIE: This government takes a very tough line on drug dealers, Lockie. And since you seem to be very chummy with Harry perhaps you should remind him of that.

LACHLAN: He doesn't deal drugs. Dad. He doesn't even use them anymore.

JAMIE: Your father couldn't intervene if Harry were to get charged and sentenced. He could face fifteen years jail. And that'd be out of our hands.

LACHLAN: Which would make things very awkward for Tom.

EGGS: Lockie. Mate. I've offered Tom a very prestigious job in Brussels.

JAMIE: And he'd be well advised to take it.

> LACHLAN *exits.*

EGGS: You don't have any scruples. Do you?

JAMIE: I leave my personal baggage at the door.

EGGS: I know. But do you ever pick it up and take it home? Look inside?

JAMIE: I don't know what you mean.

EGGS: You've got children. You love them.

JAMIE: I don't love other people's.

EGGS: No. I can see that.

◆ ◆ ◆ ◆ ◆

SCENE FIFTEEN

Tom and Angela's house.

LACHLAN: Tom! Tom!

TOM: What is it, Lock?

> LACHLAN *hands* TOM *the tea-towel.* TOM *unwraps it to expose the knife.*

This is the knife that killed Hazem? What do you want me to do?

LACHLAN: Use it. It's all you've got on him.

◆ ◆ ◆ ◆ ◆

SCENE SIXTEEN

EGGS *comes home to find* FI *packing her clothes.* FI *gets a fright.*

EGGS: What are you doing?

FI: I can't let go of him.

EGGS: What are you talking about?

FI: I can't and I won't.

EGGS: Fi.

FI: Even if you have to kill me. Have you thought of that? Have you thought of putting a pillow over my face? You may as well. Then you could get on with your glorious career. But I'm telling you—this pain I feel. This pain is the only thing that's left of my beautiful little boy. And once it's gone. There's nothing.

EGGS: Oh, my darling woman.

FI: You keep away from me. You're a poisonous brute. And I let you bully my sons. My poor little Marty. You kept pushing him. And humiliating him.

EGGS: I was toughening him up.

FI: He didn't need toughening up.

EGGS: He was going off the rails.

FI: He was only seventeen.

EGGS: No one was to blame for Marty's death except the boy himself.

FI: You've never even grieved for him. Oh, God—'Minister weeps for dead son'—you even turned that to your advantage.

EGGS: You would have preferred a scandal?

FI: Yes, damn you. I wanted the world to notice that my boy had been driven by a maniac father—driven until he died. I am not going to be the Prime Minister's wife. All right? Tom is coming for me in half an hour. So if you're planning on killing me ...

EGGS: Fiona. Ssh.

FI: ... although that hasn't made any difference with the Iraqi man. Tom knowing.

EGGS: Feeble. Ssh.

FI: Angela knows too. She told me.

EGGS: Ssh, ssh.

FI: I'm going to stay at Tom's house. I'm going to sleep in the little room out the back where Marty stayed.

EGGS: Fi. I would never hurt you. You're the reason I get up in the morning.

FI: Yeah, sure.

EGGS: I look at you now, with your eyes flashing—and I still see that wild beautiful creature flying down the slopes at Aspen.

FI: That was thirty years ago.

EGGS: I still feel the yearning for her. Praying she might notice me. Promising God that I would do anything in return if He would just give me the courage to speak to her.

FI: You were loud and brash—you just don't remember it.

EGGS: You've loved me more than I deserved. And you've loved our boys with a passion that only women know.

FI: Not enough to save him.

EGGS: Nonsense. Your love is unstoppable. I understand this in a way I've never understood before. For as long as you want, you must keep nursing our boy. Keep loving him. And loving Lachlan in the sweet way you do. And you're quite right. I have a public duty which I would like to honour. But you don't have to be part of it. In any way. We can both make our lives in whatever way we choose. You could live in Kirribilli and I could live in Canberra. I wouldn't be the first Prime Minister to make my own arrangements in Canberra. I want your happiness, Fi.

The doorbell rings.

FI: That'll be Tom.

EGGS: I was hoping we could talk a little about Martin.

FI: What do you mean?

EGGS: Just remember him, together.

FI: Tonight?

EGGS: I thought we could just… reminisce. All the little things that only you and I know.

FI: I miss him so much.

EGGS: I know.

FI: I think about him every day.

EGGS: You are such a beautiful woman.

The doorbell rings again.

FI: I should go.

EGGS: Stay. Please stay. Let me be a father.

FI: He's come specially.

EGGS: Tom wants us to be happy.

He takes her in his arms. He kisses her throat.

FI: What will I say?

EGGS: Say, 'Next week I'm going to move into the most beautiful house in this country. I am going to look out across sweeping lawns to the Harbour and the Bridge and the Opera House and I am going to be the mistress of my own life.' Tell him that. And do it quickly.

◆ ◆ ◆ ◆ ◆

SCENE SEVENTEEN

TOM *sits at the table with the knife unwrapped before him. He hears a car pulling into the drive and hastily hides the knife in a drawer.* HARRY *and* EGGS *enter.*

TOM: What is it? What's happened?

EGGS: Harry has something to tell you.

TOM: What is it, Harry?

HARRY: Dad. I think I'm in a bit of strife.

TOM: What?

ANGELA *appears in her nightie.*

ANGELA: What's going on?

EGGS: The boy's a drug addict. He's been caught on video. Fortunately for all of us, the people who nailed him aren't police.

TOM: I don't believe this. You gave me your word.

ANGELA: Stand by him, Tom.

HARRY: That Ecstasy in the car—it wasn't mine. I swear to God. I was set up.

TOM: Jesus, Harry.

HARRY: Dad. I've just been in a bit of a bad way.

ANGELA: What are you doing here, Eggs?

EGGS: I've been keeping an eye on him. More than you can say for yourself. Obviously.

TOM: I thought you had it under control.

HARRY: So did I.

ANGELA: Where were you, Harry?

HARRY: At a party. In West Melbourne.

ANGELA: [*to* EGGS] And you just happened to be passing by, did you? On your way home to Camberwell at four o'clock in the morning.

EGGS: I got a phone call.

ANGELA: From whom?

HARRY: These two thugs.

EGGS: You forget I lost my son.

ANGELA: I haven't forgotten, but I'm having trouble making the connection.

EGGS: Then you're more stupid than I thought.

ANGELA: Excuse me!

TOM: Eggs, please.

EGGS: The boy is under surveillance. Marty was the first casualty, so you'll appreciate why I'm taking a personal interest in this. You've got a problem here. A very big problem.

ANGELA: And paying thugs to rough him up is your idea of looking out for his welfare.

EGGS: I couldn't give a damn about his welfare. The only issue for you is whether I hand him over to the police.

TOM: Ange. Can you take Harry.

HARRY: I'm not dealing, Dad. I'm not.

TOM: Uh-huh. I need to talk to Eggs. Alone. Go on. Please.

ANGELA: Tom. Do whatever he wants. We can't win this. Please. I beg you. Don't let him take our boy.

    They exit.

TOM: What's this about?

EGGS: I think we both know what it's about. Loyalty.

TOM: Loyalty?

EGGS: I'm going to Canberra tomorrow morning. First thing. This is the deal: You forget about your Arab mate. Forget about the *Kelepasan*—and in exchange I leave you to do the right thing and sort out the mess with your boy.

TOM: And if I don't.

EGGS: He'll go to jail for dealing.

    Silence.

I'm sorry, Tom. I did warn you.

TOM: How has this happened to you?

EGGS: All that compassion. Where did it get you? Up shit creek. Should have taken the junket in Brussels.

    He exits. TOM *takes out the fishing knife and wipes it clean.*

◆ ◆ ◆ ◆ ◆

SCENE EIGHTEEN

EGGS *enters wearing his dark-blue suit and striped tie. He is accompanied by* FI *in a tailored suit and* LACHLAN *in his naval uniform.* FI *and* EGGS *are smiling and laughing, as he prepares to address* REPORTERS *in his new role as Prime Minister of Australia.*

EGGS: My fellow Australians. My parliamentary colleagues have done me the great and unexpected honour of choosing me as their leader. As the twenty-sixth Prime Minister of Australia, I make you this pledge: I will lead this country with honesty and integrity. In this time of global unrest, I will not flinch from a Prime Minister's most sacred duty—to defend the security of our homeland and to protect her people. And we will uphold the three great Australian principles: free markets, free speech and a fair go.

REPORTER: What will be your first act as Prime Minister?

EGGS: To take my wife Fi and my son Gunnery Officer Lachlan Benedict out for a celebratory lunch.

REPORTER: Mrs Benedict. Will you be moving into the Lodge in Canberra?

FI: No, I think the former Prime Minister has created a precedent. We'll be moving all our clobber into Kirribilli.

REPORTER: No regrets?

FI: [*laughing*] Heavens no. Kirribilli? No.

REPORTER: Gunnery Officer Benedict. As a member of our defence force, you must be pleased to have a PM who's tough on terror. Any comment?

LACHLAN *stares at the* REPORTER, *struggling with his emotions.*

FI: Lachlan?

The press conference bristles with anticipation.

EGGS: You know, my son Lockie represents a great Aussie tradition. He is one of our quiet heroes. The heir to those men and women who have led the fight against evil in two World Wars. In Korea, Vietnam and the Middle East.

And in that fight, we have learned a bitter lesson: that the forces of evil never rest—and they cannot be appeased.

My fellow Australians, we are engaged in a mighty battle for civilisation itself. And I know that the burden of sacrifice will fall most heavily on our brave service men and women. But at stake is the security of the world we hand to our children.

Tonight, the spirit of Anzac is stirring in the land. Once again, Australia is answering the call.

Blackout.

THE END

INHERITANCE
The Myrtle twins, Dibs Hamilton and Girlie Delaney, are turning 80. As the family gathers to celebrate, speculation grows as to who will inherit the family property, Allandale, when the ageing Farley Hamilton is gone. *Inheritance* is a powerful drama where duty contends with freedom, and the differences of race, gender and generation must be reconciled before the claims on Allandale, and its families, may be settled.
2 Acts—6M, 6W
9780868197203

FALLING FROM GRACE
Falling From Grace is a play with a bright comic surface and mysterious depths. It is about women in medicine, in the media and in the office—power and authority in female hands. It is also about public morality and a struggle between women to see who should be its guardian. These women are best friends in a professional world. They are witty and erudite, passionate in their pursuit of success and relentless in their pursuit of passion. They juggle careers, children and lovers. They are forty and their friendship is about to be tested.
2 Acts—2M, 5W
9780868193878

HOTEL SORRENTO
Hilary lives in seaside Sorrento with her father and sixteen-year-old son; Pippa is visiting from New York and Meg returns from England with her English husband. Three sisters, reunited after ten years in different worlds, again feel the constraints of family life. It is Meg's semi-autobiographical novel, recently short-listed for the Booker prize, which overshadows their homecoming.
'*Hotel Sorrento* is a powerful new Australian play that begins as a comedy about national identity and develops into a familial drama of great poignancy and reverberation.' Peter Craven—*Australian*
2 Acts—4M, 4W
9780868196817

LIFE AFTER GEORGE
The play that broke box office records during its Melbourne premiere season. Peter George, charismatic academic, idealist, lover of life, is dead. His wife, two ex-wives and daughter gather for his funeral. As the true nature of the man and his life unfolds, these women discover much about themselves and the lives they have lived both within and outside his shadow. *Life After George* is a moving and perceptive insight into social change across three decades told through individual experiences. From the barricades of the student movements of the late 1960s to the new century with its demands for different educational strategies, the university has been central to change. And it is on this stage that George played out his brilliant, tempestuous career.
2 Acts—2M, 4W
9780868196282